Mille Basia

Volume 2

Foreword

Somewhere in Wales 2023

Dear Readers

I have been composing Outlander Poems now for over two years, I have seen you the reader through the Drought between the series and the publication of the books.

My purpose in these compositions was and is still to raise money for the charity where I volunteer.

Riding for the Disabled.

In particular the Mount Pleasant Group and the Bridgend County Group in South Wales

This is a charity which is close to my heart. I spent a lot of my childhood and young adult life involved with horses on many levels, I rode competitively and prepared horses for competition. I was only forced to give up my equestrian endeavours due to pressure of work and family.

Once I retired, I resolved to get back involved again. The two groups where I volunteer have provided this involvement. They have taken a retiree suffering from PTSD following a career in the Police Service and made a whole human being. Restored my faith in humanity and showed me that I am worthwhile. My creative spirit was rekindled, and I resolved that I would use this to raise money for the cause.

    I started by writing short book of Horse related poetry and rhymes which were sold at various jumble sales, school fayres and other local fundraisers.

    All of this came about at the same time as the COVID pandemic. During this time, I began to re-read a book I started but did not finish on holiday many years ago. That book was Cross Stitch. Now in the guise of Outlander I read it all the way through and then discovered that it was a TV series – which I watched.

    Funny how the algorithms work – whilst perusing Facebook I came across a fan site called: Outlander Series Books and TV – I joined the group.

    I happened to post a poem which was a tongue in cheek rhyme about being addicted to Outlander and what was happening during the Drought.

    Several group members liked it and asked for another – with which I duly obliged.

    I was then encouraged to publish them in book form.

Now, many poems later I feel that I am nearing the end of the journey.

Those who have supported me on my journey this last year – my first book was published on 10th February 2021, will know, that I am my own editor in chief, my own proof-reader, and my own publicist.

I marshal assistance from several constructive critics on the Facebook page OUTLANDER SERIES BOOKS AND TV. Which is where it all started. All get a mention and a credit for their assistance in proof reading and detecting 'howlers' in my spelling, punctuation, and grammar.

I make no money personally from my efforts – any revenue generated is 100% donated to Riding for the Disabled a charity where I volunteer. RDA does amazing work with individuals suffering from a wide range of conditions, improving their quality of life, physical and mental health, and well-being.

Those who have bought and read my work may like to hear that they have funded any number of safety helmets and riding aids and are part way to a hoist for our mechanical horse Tim.

I have now covered nine of Diana's amazing novels and six series of the addictive TV show, but re-reads keep throwing up new perspectives and situations which merit attention but missed the cut in previous volumes.

I have collaborated with the amazing Lynn Fuller using her pastel drawings in my cover art – she is an amazing talent.

The cover on this occasion is courtesy of an edit by Mamaroo Designs.

This volume is the second part of a complete works of – and covers the journey of our characters from their shipwreck on the coast of America through the creation of Frasers Ridge and right up until the Mackenzie's travel back through the stones to the 1980's.

In it you will find a lot of poems which have appeared on social media and also some new ones which have been sitting in my archives.

Again, I thank Diana Gabaldon for her tolerance of my work, I hope that she feels that I at least treat her writing with respect.

I like to get inside a character's head in a situation and perhaps envisage what they may be thinking alongside what Diana wrote about a situation.

Anyway – enough of the beginning bit:

Please read on and as always have a chuckle, a weep, an occasional squirm, and most of all, enjoy.

Contents

Foreword	2
Sea Sickness	18
A verra bad sailor	20
A long Sea Voyage	22
Acupuncture	25
Ian the Wanderer	27
Marsali	29
Separate Bunks	30
The Porpoise	32
Father Fogden	34
Squeaky Noises	37
Bolt the Door	39
Jamie's Wife	41
Lord John gets it Right.	43
Ian's Rescue	45
Drowning	47
Shipwrecked	49
Season Four – oh Carolina	50
And here's some more of season four	53
Things you win at dice.	57

Burying Hayes	59
Fine Dining	61
An Offer, can I refuse?	62
Robbed	64
Bringing it all back	67
Aunt Jocasta	69
Ulysses	71
John Quincy Myers	73
The Devils Arse	75
A very noisy mule	78
Buckskins	80
Bear Killer	82
The day I killed the bear.	83
Finding the Ridge	86
What is Faith?	88
The White Sow	90
Bacon on the trot.	92
Adewayhe	94
Leaky Roof	96
Otter Tooth	98
Mrs Silversmith	100

Murtagh – ye old Coot	101
Murtagh – my godfather	103
Indecent Exposure	105
The 9th Earl – Willie	107
The Privy Council!	109
Petty Jealousy	112
Family – a mixed bunch	114
A Lass comes riding.	117
Lizzie	120
A Fish out of water	122
Two sorts of Theatre in one	126
A Verra Good Distraction.	129
Finding my father	132
A Disturbance	135
Hunting Bees	137
Not your Fault	140
Intervention	143
Termination	146
Mistaken Identity	148
Rescuing Roger	152
Father Ferigault	156

Man for man	159
My Worn-out Warrior	161
The Grimoire and the Ghost	163
Regulators	165
The Butter churn	167
My Daughter's Wedding	169
The Call to Arms	171
Horses for Courses Gideon	173
Adso	175
Warriors Prayer	177
Time and motion	179
Goats and Hell	182
Brownsville	185
Explaining Christmas	187
Christmas stockings	190
Christmas Eve	193
Christmas Morn	195
Surprise	197
Enough	200
Happy New Year	202
A Dance of Swords	203

All Life Through a Lens	205
Roger Mac and the plague of Locusts.	207
Wiley Mr Wylie	209
A hand of cards	211
The Frenchman's Gold	214
Taking Stock	216
Nine Lives	218
Attention Soldier!	220
A Coat of Red	222
Surgeons Kit	225
A Ghoistidh,	227
Godson	229
Breathe Again!	231
Astrolabe	233
Shadows in the Hearth	236
The Knack of being married.	238
The Hayloft.	240
Down wind	243
Bitten by a Snake	245
Snake Bite	248
Maggots and Leeches	251

Death's door	254
Choosing Life	256
My Buffalo Gals	258
Flashback to Ardsmuir	261
The Family Christie	263
A Broken Family	265
Major MacDonalds Wig	268
Dr Rawlins Casebook	270
Understanding Women	272
Myrtle Berries	275
Tulach Ard	277
Grand Da has Balls	280
Stones of Ardsmuir	282
Fisher Folk	284
Coming Home	287
A restless night	289
Making Hay	291
Goodbye Iseabail	294
The Call of Faith	296
Anaesthetics	297
The Devils Genes	299

Matches	301
Understanding Men	303
Malva	305
The Devils Pact	306
Pain Relief	307
The Right Hand of the Lord	309
The Ballad of James McCready	311
Loneliness of men	314
Rape	316
Brave Wee Thing	319
Faithfulness	321
Over Your Shoulder	323
Little Boxes	325
I've Taken no Such Oath	328
The Mask of Sleep	330
Come Back Sassenach	333
One Hand	335
Fergus Man!!	338
Mother Claire	340
Master of Mushrooms	342
Resurrection	344

Mixed Metaphors	346
Beware of the Pig!!	347
Calls in the Forest – a Cry for Help	349
Trail of Tears	351
Kiss them better.	353
The Venom of the North Wind.	355
Desecration	357
Calling Roger Mac	359
Continental Congress	361
A White Rose for the British	363
Light relief	366
Talking Ballocks	368
Aldwych Farce	370
The Wind of War	372
Unrest	374
Tar brush and Bucket	376
Tar and feathers	378
Twenty Rifles	381
Boys will be Boys.	383
The Blazing Shits	385
Fever	387

Scales of pain	389
Sorcha	391
A Cool Haircut	393
He floats.	395
Wisdom of Solomon	397
Faecal matter	400
Mortality	402
Seeing Double	405
Unconventional	407
Gallberry Ointment	409
Keeping a lid on things	411
Unholy Trinity	413
Lessons in the snow	415
Chaos in the Kitchen	416
Head lice	418
Dear Jamie/Dear John	420
The Plan	422
A Warped Mind	424
Shamed	426
Superstition	428
Toil and Trouble	430

Ringing in the Ears	433
Trouble in Spades	435
A Moments Rest	437
Bolt the Door – again	439
Rough Justice	441
Scales of Justice	443
Surety	446
Taken	448
Gone	450
I fight with you	452
Bodies on the Beach	453
Staying Alive	455
He will come Today	457
The Jamie Fraser guide to Prisons	460
Listening from the kitchen	462
Get out of my kitchen	464
Burgers for Tea	467
Spaghetti Tree	469
A side of chips too far	471
PB & J	473
Dreamscape	475

Forbes Ear	477
Talisman	479
Mistress Forbes Picnic	481
Chowder and Marching	483
A verra English Uncle	485
Meeting on the Dock	487
Blood will out	489
Unrepentant	492
Conspiracy Theory	495
Michael Mouse	498
Telephone for Grand Da	500
Lost Soul Remembered	502
Home Raiders	505
Sworn Vengeance	508
The Coming Storm	510
Jamie and Claire's Theme	511
Acknowledgements	513
Copyright	513
Other work by the author	514

Leaving Scotland 1766

Sea Sickness

A wilted heap of blankets,
Heaped upon the bed,
The green tinged groaning monster,
Could hardly raise its head.

Go away, the only words,
To anyone who asked,
The straining, heaving reflex.
Barely even masked.

Nothing stayed inside him,
His stomached had rebelled,
The sight of sour pickles,
Its wrath would not be quelled.

Try the Chinese remedy.
We heard the same reply.
The pair of you should go away,
Leave me here to die.

Vomiting will burn your throat,
Put your insides through the mangle.
Will tear your inner muscles.
cause your testicles to tangle.

Should that last thing happen?
There only is one cure,
I would have to cut them off,
Of that You can be sure

From deep under the blankets,
A leg emerging first,
Stick me with yer golden pins!
Willoughby do yer worst,

I'll have tae trust ye Sassenach.
For my balls I'll not be grieving,
And Willoughby goes o'er the side.
If this does nae stop the heaving

A verra bad sailor

With eyes on the horizon
I try and hold my thoughts.
The wooden deck below my feet,
A coffin lid of sorts,

The endless bobbing up and down,
Is churning up my wame,
I'd rather die than be here.
If that's all the same.

Turning green around the gills,
Is not good for my pride,
I feel my breakfast rising,
Must it leap out o'er over the side,

Lying down or standing up,
Above deck or below,
I can'nae stop from puking,
Is there nowhere else tae go.

Living with a bucket
Fast between yer feet,
Three months with no solid ground,
Is really quite a feat.

Or I must suffer needles,
Poked into my head,
Looking like a porcupine,
Or taking to my bed.

Those little golden needles,
Surely do their work,
Even if the look of them
Makes me feel a burke,

Sassenach I am all yours,
Take me – do your worst,
But stop the world from spinning,
And the deck from plunging first.

Stick me with yer golden pins,
Feed me with yer tea,
And swear this is the last time,
I shall ever cross the sea.

A Long Sea Voyage

We've travelled far across the sea,
Me and yer granny Claire,
Ye'll ken she's said how sick I get,
Just smelling salty air.

We had a big adventure,
Finding yer cousin Ian
Yes – the one who is a Mohawk Brave,
Sit down ye cheeky wean.

On a ship the Artemis,
Owned by my cousin Jared,
Yes – the one who sold the wine,
The one who lived in Paris.

Settle down now, listen,
Or I'll pack ye off to bed.
If ye keep on interruptin'
List to what I've said.

The Artemis a sturdy ship,
Powered then by sails,
Her crew were superstitious ay,
So, we touched the horse shoe nails.

Then the wind stopped blowing,
She stopped – we were becalmed.
Running out of water,
Would we keep out of harm.

Wily Mr Willoughby,
Chinese – have I told.
I found him sleeping on the dock.
In Scotland in the cold.

Yi Tien Cho – his real name,
Leans against heaven.
A courtier from the Chinese court.
Skilled in Chinese medicine.

He cured me of the seasickness.
With needles long and fine
Stuck at places in my heid.
Just like a porcupine!

He had been writing poems,
A story of his life,
He threw them all over the side,
The wind came back to life,

This satisfied the sailors,
And it was not to be,
They shelved a plan, to throw a man.
For luck, into the sea.

Wily little Willoughby
Watched the birds you see,
When they fly low to the water,
A breath of wind will be.

When the birds are flying high,
The upper air is calm.
No wind about to fill the sails.
The sailors need a charm.

Rain came down to fill the kegs.
We had our fill of water.
And set off for Jamaica,
With more sail than we ought a.

Next, I'll tell of Granny Claire
She had adventures too.
As Doctor on a seventy-four.
Healing all the crew.

I can see ye sleeping,
Go quietly to yer beds.
Crawl under yer covers
And rest ye weary heads.

Acupuncture

I'd been throwing up for days,
I did not feel verra well,
I'd drunk a lot of ginger tea,
And still I felt like hell.

I cannot sleep for heaving,
If I eat, I chuck it,
Ye cannot feel like living.
With yer head inside a bucket

Willoughby is a strange one,
Keeps hit talents hid,
Says he has a Chinese cure,
If I do as he bids.

He produced a box of needles,
Thin and made of gold,
Where was he going to stick them,
That thought sent me cold.

I look like a porcupine,
I don't ken what that is,
Must be a rare, strange animal,
With a face that looks like this!

But on the morrow, I am not green.
I'm not puking in the sea.
I'll break it to Claire gently.
That I din'nae need her Tea.

Ian the Wanderer

Redcoats raided Lallybroch.
The day that I was born.
They'd heard the sound of gunfire.
From the farm that very morn.

I was in my uncle Jamie's arms.
Him a wanted man ye ken
His face the first I ever saw.
I think we bonded then.

My name is Ian Murray
They named me for my da.
But I'm more like my uncle.
I am Fraser to the core.

My ma just wants to keep me close.
I'm the youngest of her flock.
She thinks I'll stay upon the farm.
With Da and be his rock.

I want to go adventuring.
I've grown up, I'm not a child.
Ma would keep me on her apron strings.
It's driving me quite wild.

I've run away to Uncle Jamie
He's had to take me back.
And then I get a thrashing
My arse is beaten blue and black.

He followed to Jamaica.
When I was kidnapped by a ship
To take me back home to ma
If I survived the trip.

If I had'nae been kidnapped
There would be no Frasers Ridge
We would na have left Scotland.
I think they're glad we did.

When I stayed with the Indians
It made me the man I am.
I've learned to live a simple life.
I am a simple man.

Highlander and Mohawk
I had an Indian wife.
When I had to leave her
It was the worst time of my life.

I'm tied to Uncle Jamie
With him I always have a home
He is the star which guides me.
Wherever I should roam.

Marsali

Mother, wife, companion,
Lover, critic, friend,
Feisty, smart, unstoppable,
Faithful! To the end.

Run away from Scotland.
To be with who you love,
Caring, funny, tolerant,
But not a setting dove,

Patient! and compassionate
Daughter of a wench
Putting up with Fergus
Who is very very French,

Raised as Jamie's daughter.
Not too fussed on Claire,
But loves her as a mother.
Now that Laoghaire is not there.

Separate Bunks

I will na have ye sharing,
She is nae yet yer wife,
Handfast does nae cut it,
Her mother will cause strife.

There is nae point in begging,
And din nae think I'm blind.
Fergus ye will share with me,
I will na' change ma mind.

Marsali shall sleep with Claire,
Until we find a priest,
Ye will have vows, if not in church,
Ye will do that at least.

Canoodling in corners,
Love amidst the ropes,
No privacy is found at sea,
So don't build up your hopes,

My cabin mate thinks me a witch,
Or at the best a whore,
At least I have the biggest berth,
I hope she doesn't snore.

Fergus is frustrated,
Marsali hates my guts,
Sleeping without Jamie
The lack will drive me nuts.

Sassenach, contain yer lust,
I've aching in my crotch,
I'll meet ye on the afterdeck,
When they change the watch

The Porpoise

You don't argue with a seventy-four,
She could blow us out the water,
Jamie's protests all for naught,
We have to, like we ought ter!

Bound also for Jamaica,
She wasn't pressing crew,
There was a form of plague on board.
A doctor was their due.

So, I went aboard the Porpoise,
Its crew were full of fever,
Typhoid is a killer,
I knew I couldn't leave her.

A quiet lad, he does his job,
A helper I have found,
At 14 in the Navy,
God bless Elias Pound.

Intelligent and helpful,
With quiet and shrewd remark
Helps to keep the crew alive,
He really made his mark.

The fever cured, the ship now clean.
The crew regained some pride,
Elias Pound lay down to sleep,
And in his sleep, he died.

I sewed Elias in his shroud,
White from head to toes,
Tucked in his lucky rabbit's foot.
And put the last stitch through his nose.

Father Fogden

Brave or really stupid,
I'd jumped into the sea,
Floated with the current,
To a beach, and I was free.

Where was I? I had not a clue?
This plan was really daft.
To get me to Jamaica,
First, I must find a craft.

I wandered in the jungle,
Was bitten bad by ants,
No water and no sunscreen,
This holiday is pants!

I came round tied down to a bed!
My legs were sorely itching,
What is this place, it's really weird,
My get out button is twitching.

He's talking to a coconut!
He asks it for advice,
It says that I can't leave too soon,
Cos the weathers not too nice.

This man of some religion,
Has really lost his marbles,
Must be the hemp he's smoking,
Makes him really garbled.

But there is a wreck upon the shore,
A sailor killed his goat,
A little slant eyed Chinese man,
That Willoughby, I thought.

And there they were, on the beach.
Just packing up and leaving,
I might just catch the Artemis,
But distance is deceiving.

I wave and shout, he cannot hear.
I will be left behind.
But he sees my signal flash,
Thank God my loves not blind!

Father Fogden held a wedding,
For a couple on the sand,
The form a bit impromptu,
The sentiment quite grand.

Father Fogden is a strange man.
Of that there is no doubt,
But he blessed us too,
In his own way,

His faith still quite devout.

Squeaky Noises

Why is it that they scratch their balls?
It's just because they can!
Naked in their universe,
Just being a man.

Curious shades of body hair,
Add a touch of spice,
And when you've been three months at sea,
Don't forget the lice!

Beards can be such sensual things,
Erotic to the touch,
Don't make plans to shave just yet,
I've planned for this so much,

Not half of what I've planned for you,
Ye maker of wee sounds,
When I get you on the shore, alone.
I shall make ye howl like hounds!

Hot water and some vinegar,
You're having a good scrub,
Keep your infestation,
Confined to the tub.

I'll have ye lie a top o me,
Yer arse I love tae squeeze,
I've not had room tae do these things,
Since we've been on the seas,

A soapy kiss, a testing grope,
His touch is all allure,
He's smelling more like Jamie now,
Much less like a sewer,

Now Captain of the Artemis,
Before we put to sea,
Plans reclamation of his wife,
The sound effects come free!

Louse free, scrubbed, and shiny,
Anticipating pleasure,
Shall I take him somewhere very quiet,
And scratch his balls at leisure!

Bolt the Door
At sea 1766

Fevered drunk and horny,
Best describes the scene,
My Captain making light of it,
He tries to keep it clean,

Cramped up in the cabin,
No room to swing a cat,
There are somethings I'd rather swing,
I'm very sure of that.

Too weak to wield a needle.
I can't inject my bum.
My Captain is quite squeamish,
With the plunger 'neath his thumb.

Hotter than the fires of hell,
My skin aflame to touch,
Light of head, and addled mind,
He's not expecting much.

I will possess his body,
I know he will come round,
This fevered witch will have her way,
And never make a sound.

My mind surveys the table,
Or should we use the floor,
In between the furniture,
Different for sure.

Heavy on the Sherry,
It has the right effect,
A steaming aphrodisiac,
And I will not object.

Turtle soup, delicious
I could eat some more.
Then I'll tell the captain,
He'd better bolt the door.

Jamie's Wife

For all those years he yearned for her,
But only said she'd gone,
Out of sight not out of mind,
Her memory was strong.

He talked about her seldom,
With words of loss and chill
A man whose soul bore one great hole.
That only she could fill.

Now she walks beside him,
Not just a pretty face
A beauty rare, and singular
That time will not erase,

Intelligent, most certainly,
Not some bit of fluff,
I might have known that Jamie's wife.
Is made of sterner stuff.

Erudite and courteous,
But not afraid to flirt,
Secure in the knowledge.
That he'll not be chasing skirt,

Do I detect a green streak,
Yes, she's jealous of my time,
That I had his company,
But he was never mine.

Amber eyes see through me,
Protective of her man,
A face of glass can't hide her thoughts,
And neither can her fan.

Why John tis good tae see ye,
His voice raises my hair.
And may I introduce my wife,
Lord John Grey, meet Claire.

Lord John gets it Right.

Governor of Jamaica,
Seems a fair promotion,
Just five thousand miles away,
A mere hop across an ocean.

My welcoming reception,
I'm dressed up in full fig.
When I spot Jamie Fraser,
And what is that? a wig!

Much as I admire the man,
He's always bringing trouble,
Ah – here come HMs marines,
At the bloody double.

He is again a wanted man,
But they've no written proof,
No warrant to arrest him,
I'm thinking on the hoof.

The ambitious little upstart,
With only acting rank,
Who comes to take him prisoner,
Is a nuisance if I'm frank.

I pull out my best disdain,
And put him in to the test.
Leftenant! When not on your ship
Where's your power to arrest.

Your power is only out at sea,
It ended on the dock,
Now kindly leave my friend alone,
You jumped up little cock!!

Ian's Rescue

We landed in Jamaica.
Storm swept, bruised, and battered,
The Artemis dis masted,
Hers sails mostly in tatters.

With Jamie on the wanted list,
We must avoid the Navy,
And that temporary Captain.
Who is dishing out the gravy.

Is Ian on the Island,
Taken as a slave,
Our mission is to find him,
Before he meets his grave.

The Governors reception
Moves our mission on,
A get out of jail free card,
Written by Lord John.

What is Geillis Duncan
Doing on this Isle,
A good three husbands later
She's doing it in style.

The cave was called Abandawe,
It's a portal like the stones,
Ian was her sacrifice,
She'd turn him into bones.

She would not take my nephew,
I'd guard him with my life,
It was me that took her head off.
With a sugar cutting knife

Drowning

A wave as high as all the masts
Swept me o'er the side,
Snagged on the metal from a spar,
I really should have died,

Floating down, endless peace,
I could not fight the feeling,
Embrace the everlasting light,
A wondrous sense of healing,

Just breathe in, and all is well.
Fold the swell around you,
And God will put your earthly soul.
Right back where he found you.

The feeling breaks, the rope is cut.
I'm held in his embrace,
Breath is shared, his and mine,
Upwards now we race.

I had the choice to take that breath,
It would have been my last
Drowning is a peaceful way,
To make peace with your past.

Twas he who would not let me leave,
Twas he who gave me breath.
His love for me will never see.
Me meet a watery death.

Shipwrecked

Washed up on a distant shore.
The ship around us broken.
Strewn on sand, where is this land,
The land that God has chosen.

I don't know why I'm breathing,
I'm pretty sure I drowned,
A never-ending weightlessness,
Then Jamie all around.

Are there more survivors,
Or are we the only two.
Have we lost all our family?
Is there only me and you.

Yes, there were survivors,
And our bedraggled band,
Had reached the coast of Georgia,
God had had a hand.

Scotland seems so long ago.
Oh, so far away,
Time to see what lies in store.
We've reached the USA.

Season Four – oh Carolina

So here I am still writing.
And here comes season four.
We've reached the Carolinas.
The Frasers are on Tour!

Meanwhile in obsession land
I've started eating Parritch.
I don't really want the problem.
King Louis had in Paris.

The spare room has been fitted out.
With stone walls and bars and chains
My husband is responsible.
He always takes such pains.

I'm not sure of his motives.
Oh Lord John! What can I say?
I think he's got it mixed up.
With fifty shades of grey.

Less of my domestic strife
Let's get back to the plot.
Things don't go well for our friend Hayes.
But Bonnet skips the knot!

Never fall for Irish charm
Or as they call it Blarney.
Bonnet is a wicked man.
Jamie you were Barmy.

Robbed of all except their clothes
Claire's rings are swallowed twice.
Young Ian has acquired a dog.
Rollo – he won him playing dice.

River Run is quite a pad.
Jocasta a MacKenzie
She needs a man to run the show.
She could leave the lot to Jamie.

But Claire is anti-slavery.
This is a deal breaker.
Jamie isn't all that keen.
He doesn't try to make her.

A deal is done with Tryon.
For an acreage of land
I think it's big as the whole of Wales.
That's where they make their stand.

Meanwhile back in our time
Brianna makes a find.
Her parents' death, an epitaph
They both die in a fire.

She leaves a note for Roger.
And heads off for the stones.
Hoping to warn her parents.
That they may not make 'old bones'

Meanwhile up on Frasers ridge
The Indians call around.
Seems Scots and Native Indians
Can share a common ground.

A cabin built for shelter.
Some livestock and a bed
A fight with a half crazed Indian Bear
That's how Fraser life is led.

Meanwhile Roger finds the note.
And goes in search of Bree.
And meets with Captain Bonnet
And journeys across the sea.

They all end up in Wilmington.
Including dopey Lizzie
Hold on to your kilts my friends.
The next half will be busy.

And here's some more of season four.

It's all been very hectic.
I'm still in season four.
Rogers with the Mohawk
That won't end well, I'm sure.

The Frasers pack the wagon.
Take Bree to River Run
Rogers walking far to New York.
He's not having so much fun.

Jamie, Claire, and Ian
Mount up and off they go.
To try and buy our Roger back.
I hope it doesn't snow.

Meanwhile I've acquired.
A doorstop highland Coo
A tin of Highland Shortbread
And a dress that's nearly new.

My sword is still hung on the wall.
My Dirk is by the fire.
Along with a large sheepskin rug
An object of desire.

My husband's brandishing his belt.
I don't think he wants to thank me.
I've strengthened up my throwing arm.
In case he tries to spank me.

Brianna reads the letter.
Jamie left with Lord John Grey
I talk about forgiveness.
She takes it the wrong way.

Bonnet has been captured.
He's languishing in prison.
Bree gets Lord John to take her there.
And Bonnet is forgiven.

But some the regulators also
Are locked up in the jail.
They need to get their people out.
And with a plan that cannot fail....

They blow the bloody doors off
The jail in just a minute
Leaving but a pile of wood
And Bonnet .... Isn't in it.

Meanwhile up in New York State
Things have gone astray.
They've rescued Roger from the tribe.
But Young Ian has to stay.

Rogers in a quandary
Claire's told him about Bree.
Will he make a commitment?
Or run off home …… we'll see.

And so, they're back at River Run
And the baby has arrived.
Brees got engaged to good Lord John
To avoid what Jocasta has contrived.

When the Frasers get there
Travelling without Ian
Brees waiting there for Roger.
But he's not come ……read on

The Frasers have packed the wagon.
And they're leaving for the ridge.
Oh look – here comes Roger.
Riding 'cross the bridge.

June 1767

Things you win at dice.

I was in a bar in Wilmington.
Tied up to a wall.
My owner was playing dice.
And losing – I recall

I had my head down on my paws.
But I wasn't asleep.
My ear was cocked and listening.
In case I had to leap.

I'd never had an owner.
Keep me more than a few days.
I'm half a dog and half a wolf.
With antisocial ways.

Oh, here comes my new one.
He's nothing but a lad.
He seems to be quite proud of me.
Things can't be all that bad

He's going to call me Rollo
Rollo of the dice.
I've never had a name before
I think that's really nice.

Oooh, he has a family.
This is what I need.
They know I can catch my own fish.
I'm really cheap to feed.

Now I am a Fraser.
The Frasers are my pack.
Ian is my master.
I'm never looking back.

Burying Hayes

Hayes was dead, I saw him hanged.
At his last he saw a friend,
So full up wi whisky
He did'na feel the end.

A superstitious bugger
He feared the dark at best.
The churchyard was the proper place.
To lay his bones to rest.

We gave him a fair send off.
In the Gaelic sung some songs
With his body in the wagon
Left Charleston to the throng.

The Priest had wanted to pay,
Of flesh he'd have his pound,
To rest a sinner like old Hayes
In consecrated ground.

'Twas dusk when we left Charleston.
A shovel had been bought.
We picked a spot beside the wall.
That Hayes would like, we thought.

He was hiding in my wagon,
Still fettered up for hanging,
Scairt Young Ian witless,
When his chains they started clanging.

He talked the talk; he was a thief.
But a friend of Hayes, ye ken
Condemned to hang for smuggling.
And I was taken in.

By candle light we dug his grave,
We didn't tell the priest,
Buried him and said a prayer.
At rest now at least,

Hayes now safely in the ground
We must resume our journey,
The wagon should be empty now.
Not acting as a gurney.

He talked me into freeing him,
I would not hand him in,
Shook my hand and thanked me.
And parted with a grin.

I miss judged the Irish bastard,
With his easy line in charm.
I should have seen it in his eyes.
He only meant us harm.

Fine Dining

Invited out to dinner,
Dining in fine style,
A chance to sell an asset,
And network for a while,

I'm sitting at a table,
Am I mutton dressed as lamb,
Finest wares out on display,
Please pass another clam!

Men in conversation
Take a closer look,
The ruby hanging round my neck,
Really was the hook.

Dangled in no setting.
Except the wearers skin,
This flawless stone was guaranteed.
To draw a buyer in.

The sale negotiated,
We've gold then in our purse,
Will we find our destiny,
Or suffer something worse.

An Offer, can I refuse?

I've an offer Mr Fraser,
The land needs such as you,
Men to colonise this land,
Men to keep order too.

Land where you could prosper,
Ye know, I know your aunt,
Fertile land a plenty,
And the power of grant.

Governor, I have read the law,
I really do not see,
How the Kings conditions
Can apply to me.

Male and white and Protestant
Thirty years of age,
This is written down as law,
I've seen it on the page.

I can nae take yer offer,
I will nae find a spot.
I'm Male and white and of that age.
But Protestant I am not!

Sit and take a brandy,
Tryon poured the large,
The offers there, negotiate.
Before you catch the barge.

Northern Carolina
Needs the like of you.
Unafraid to take a risk,
Or stretch a law or two.

Would be a shame to turn it down,
The acreage is great,
Ten thousand in the back lands,
You'd have plenty on your plate.

We are far from London,
You are troubling no one.
And you see there is the Law.
And then there's what is done.

Robbed

All aboard the Sally Anne,
She headed up the river,
Despite the lack of any waves,
Jamie's insides were aquiver.

All of our belongings
Were loaded on this boat,
Nothing else here to our name,
I hope we stay afloat.

The river seems so peaceful.
Lush ground on either side,
All of mother nature
Undisturbed, as on we glide.

A beautiful and wild land,
Where anyone may roam,
Four travellers and a half wolf dog,
Where will we find a home.

At dusk, we tied up for the night.
We thought it safe from harm,
Twas Rollo's growl and barking
Sounded the alarm.

They stormed the cabin in a mob.
Even Jamie could not fight.
Knife to his throat, four pinned him down,
Struggle as he might.

They knew we had some money,
They searched him to his skin.
Found what they were looking for,
And then did not give in.

What they did not take they broke,
My surgeons kit and things
The leader of these vile men
Tried to steal my rings.

I took them off quite gracefully.
And held them in his sight.
Then rammed them hard into my mouth.
And swallowed them in fright.

I bit his hand as it searched my mouth.
His fingers on my tongue,
He made me spit the rings back out.
But I had swallowed one.

The one he stole meant all to me.
But wasn't worth a lot.
Twas the Iron one, from Jamie
From the key to Lallybroch.

I recognised that Irish brogue.
His voice an evil sonnet,
I would not forget that night.
At the hands of Stephen Bonnet

We arrived at Aunt Jocasta's,
With nothing to our name.
But the clothes that we stood up in,
And the will to start again.

Bringing it all back

Bonnets gang stole all we had,
We are back again to nought,
My wedding ring I'd swallowed,
How to retrieve it? I'd not thought.

I could feel it stuck there,
A lump, hard in my throat,
Only two ways out of there,
Not pleasant on a boat.

Why does he want the captain's pipe,
He seems to have a plan,
Some water, and a bucket,
Aggravating man.

I've seen that look upon his face,
Mischievous intent,
I'm not going to like this much,
I know when he's hell bent!

Tipped into the beaker,
The scrapings from the pipe
Burnt tobacco, ash, and all.
He gave its bowl a wipe.

It floated on the water,
The look of it! The stink!
He fixed me with 'obey me' eyes,
And ordered me to drink.

I shook my head, I would not!
The taste would be too vile,
A strong arm reached around me,
He grasped me with a smile.

That Scottish bastard held my nose,
He prised open my mouth,
Then that bloody sadist,
Poured the liquid south!

I heaved and retched; my face turned red.
I swallowed then, oh F*@k it!
My stomach contents ring and all
Spewed into the bucket!

I'll have you, Jamie Fraser!
I'm still heaving from that brew,
My insides trying to get out,
And you enjoyed it too!

It's better that way Sassenach.
He held his sides with laughter,
If it went through the other way,
Ye'd have tae find it – after!

Aunt Jocasta

Don't be fooled by Aunt Jocasta,
She's Mackenzie through and through,
She'll walk you down her winding path.
And her will she'll have you do.

There's always an agenda,
Hiding in the wings,
A wee wee scorpion hiding there,
A most poisonous of stings.

But she is my kinfolk,
I have to play along,
Until the bit where I get hit,
Then things may go wrong.

When she lost her daughters,
They were on the run,
The gold under the carriage,
Is what built River Run.

She wants to leave an empire,
Legacy, she craves.
But I'll not be having anything,
Built on the back of slaves.

I cannot think I'll of her,
She is lonely, needs a man,
She knows she can'nae move my mind.
I have my own plan.

The Mackenzie blood is deep in her,
She schemes just like her brother,
I cannot see it all as fault,
She looks just like my mother.

Ulysses

I am more than just a servant,
Answering her call,
More than just the Butler
Standing by the wall.

I know the darkest secrets,
This family keeps tight,
I know the grief Jocasta keeps,
Hidden from your sight.

She marries for protection,
Never more for love,
And I will be here by her side,
Black hand in a white glove,

I am her eyes; I see for her.
I watch while she holds court,
I would give my life for her,
Without a second thought.

She plans and she manipulates,
She tries to get her way,
When all she wants is family,
And she wants them all to stay.

There is a sadness in her life,
Which can't be cured by gold.
A fear of being left alone,
Blind and growing old.

I will never leave her,
And no - I'm not a slave,
I love the woman desperately,
I'm Ulysses the brave.

John Quincy Myers

We meet him first at River Run
A back woods man alright.
With a hairy face and hairy back
He looks a real sight.

A Welshman with a heart of gold
He lives up in the hills.
Trading with the Indians
Using his trapping skills.

A friend of Aunt Jocasta
He knows his way around.
Teaches Ian about the Mohawk tribe.
Helps the Frasers find their ground.

Handy with a scrubbing brush
He gets Rollo smelling sweet.
After tangling with that skunk
He scrubbed him up a treat.

We almost lost John Myers
When he tangled with that bear
Though it was really human
It gave him quite a scare.

Wounded and bedraggled.
With a big rip in his Britches
Don't you worry readers.
Claire will soon have him in stitches

The Devils Arse

What is that strange thing Auntie?
He chased it through the grass.
Twas black and white and feisty
And stinks like the devil's arse,

I'm glad he did nae catch it,
Or at least he let it go,
It's bad enough he smells so bad.
I'm sorry Auntie Jo.

Uncle Jamie where's yer gun,
We need tae shoot this beast.
I'll never get the scent out,
It needs tae be deceased!

Best we move ourselves outside.
Breakfast in the air,
And Ian goes and bathe that dog,
I think that's only fair.

See John Quincy Myers
He'll tell ye what ye need,
Soak your hound in vinegar.
Of stench he will be freed

Will ye all stop laughing.
I'd swear ye all are drunk.
Rollo that's the last time.
Ye'll be tanglin wi a skunk!

Into the Wilderness
August 1767

A very noisy mule

I miss my days at River Run,
Life was quiet there,
I was a favourite of the mistress,
A mule without a care.

As loud a mule as you will find,
With a voice to raise the dead,
A loyal and a kindly mule,
As long as I get fed!

She gave me to her nephew,
That fiery red-haired Scot,
He loads me up with boxes,
He makes me work a lot.

They took me through the forest,
There was thunder and then lightening,
I took off and ran away,
That storm was really frightening.

I am a sort off homing mule,
I came back in the morning,
My bray was heard for miles around,
As the day was dawning.

I've was stolen by the teamsters,
I bit one in the arm,
That very rough man bit me back,
He really had no charm.

I should have been a Fraser,
I'm as stubborn as the boss,
I like to stand right on his foot,
That makes him really cross.

Now I live with Fergus,
As I'm getting rather old.
We have an understanding,
And I never will be sold.

Buckskins

What is that strange garment?
She is nae wearing stays,
I quite like the joggling!
It's a brassiere she says.

To ride into the mountains,
She will'na wear a dress,
Or ride there like a lady,
Aye! she means tae cause me stress.

She's made a pair of breeches,
They cling there is no doubt,
All the world will see her arse,
I can'nae let her out.

I ken that if her mind is fixed,
Reason comes to nought,
She says she's watched my arse for years,
Without impure thought!

Now if I was tae wear the kilt,
She'd ravish me for sure,
She knows just what her whiles will do,
My thoughts are now impure.

I feel her flesh beneath the cloth,
Warm and round and firm,
Shall I remove these buckskin pants?
Then I could make her squirm,

Infuriating Sassenach,
Too well ye know my mind,
I love tae watch ye joggling,
I love yer round behind.

I'll let ye have ye wardrobe,
I have no choice of course,
But the only thing yer sitting on,
'Cept me, will be yer horse!

Bear Killer

Horses hobbled for the night,
A view fit to admire.
We thought to cook the fish I'd caught.
And lie down by the fire.

It came out of the bushes,
Beady eyes a gleaming,
Lips pulled back to show its teeth,
Drool from its muzzle streaming.

I just had time to grab my dirk.
And push Claire out the way,
When dense black fur ran over me,
I thought it was my day,

Savage teeth, raking claws,
Its smell was fit to choke!
I wrestled for my life with it,
In its rage at being awoke.

Then smack! The world went silver.
I let out a shout,
My ever helpful, loving wife,
Had hit me with a trout.

The day I killed the bear.

Where's my old plaid Sassenach,
I hope ye have nae thrown it,
I've only worn it thirty years,
If there's holes, you could ha' sewn it.

Ah there it is, now let's sit down.
Get comfy in my chair,
I'll tell you of the very night,
I fought and killed a bear.

Twas before we had the land ye ken.
Just me and Granny Claire,
Travelled through the mountains,
Looking for a home to share.

We found a place to spend the night,
Camping by a stream,
I was cooking fish we'd caught.
When I heard her scream.

It came out of the bushes,
Its beady eyes were gleaming,
Its claws were long as short swords.
Foam from its mouth was streaming,

I dropped the fish; I grabbed my knife.
And as swiftly as I dare.
I pushed your granny out the way,
And wrestled with the bear.

The thick black fur was fit to choke,
I stank of something foul,
It's claws it sank into my back,
It really made me howl.

I'd never fought a beast this strong,
Armed only with a knife,
If I couldn't kill it verra soon,
The bear would end my life.

I stabbed and slashed,
It tried to bite; its breath was in my ear.
It pinned me down, the world went black,
My time was up I fear,

I felt my knife pierce through its hide,
I heard the rip of skin,
I smelled the blood, and stink of bear,
I think I might just win,

I pushed myself up to my feet,
I prayed and made a wish,
And then yer very helpful granny
Hit me with the fish.

Are ye listening Sassenach,
You've an arm tae swing a trout.
A fish is not a weapon.
But you fair near knocked me out!

Finding the Ridge

We couldn't live with owning slaves,
We turned down River Run,
Aunt Jocasta would soon find.
A man to her business done.

We'd take up on a land grant,
But that would come with strings.
Tryon wanted military men,
Amongst other things.

We headed for the mountains,
To find a patch of land,
A place where we could put down roots,
A place to make a stand.

Sheltered in the woodland.
Not far from a stream
Fish and game in plenty,
It was a settler's dream,

And emerging from the forest,
Its beauty made me shiver,
Trees as far as the eye could see,
flat land along the river.

My farmers eye loved everything,
It had a special feel,
And finding Fraser strawberries,
Seemed to seal the deal.

We'd need to sign the papers.
And mark out all the ground.
A great big patch of paradise
Frasers Ridge was found.

What is Faith?

It is not just observing.
the ritual of the church
Faith is holding a belief,
a vision of its worth,

The ceremonial service.
The formal observation
Is there to focus all your thoughts.
To aid your meditation,

A priest is but a conduit,
He helps to spread the word,
And shares the burden of your sin.
With each confession heard,

Belief that there is purpose.
Belief in man's endeavour
Belief in your eternal soul
Is faith you hold forever.

Faith does not need a building,
Faith does not need a priest.
Faith does not need religious cant.
All faith needs is belief.

Faith will guide your actions,
Faith will heal your soul.
When all is lost, and hope is gone.
Faith will keep you whole.

Living with a man of faith
Is difficult at times,
For he believes that one true being
Absolves him of his crimes.

His faith in his ability
To walk his chosen path,
Will surely take us journeying.
A long way from our hearth.

My faith is much more simple,
I don't act on a whim,
I consider all pertinent facts.
And then have faith in him.

The White Sow

She was the dearest piglet,
Wriggly and pink.
But always up to mischief,
She quickly learned to think.

We kept her longer than we should,
For we were quite mistaken,
That she would join our family.
That pig should have been bacon.

A streak of independence.
Every day she would escape,
Leaving a trail of destruction.
And carnage in her wake.

The list of things she's eaten
Is getting quite impressive.
Jamie's hat, Brianna's drawers,
That pig gets more aggressive.

Growing bigger every day,
Now with piglets of her own,
She got to choose just where she went.
Or her wrath would soon be known.

She does exactly as she likes,
She scares the pants of men,
No amount of food enticement
Will keep her in a pen.

Even the Indians respect her.
The white sow from the ridge,
I'm sure she'd have been bacon.
If we'd only had a fridge.

Bacon on the trot.

I was born I know not where,
To market I was taken,
Sold to the highest bidder,
Destined to be bacon.

I love my food; I hate my pen.
Those humans are mistaken,
If they think I'll hang around,
And let them make me bacon.

I'm living in the pantry,
Surrounded by their food,
If I decide to eat it all,
That would be seen as rude.

Piglets come and piglets go.
I give them all the talk,
Tell them they should run away,
Before they become pork.

I've found a warm and cosy den,
Down in the foundation
No one dare come near me,
I've bred bacon for the nation.

I've a very simple attitude
When it comes to men,
Eat them or get eaten.
My meat is not for them.

Adewayhe

Her face
Is worn by life and time.
weathered by the years,
A mantle worn with quiet pride,
With the wisdom of the Seers.

Her Eyes
Deep pools of darkness,
A stillness filled with light,
All seeing, and all knowing,
Through time she has the sight.

Her smile
A peaceful blessing,
A calmness sure and true,
She reads the soul before her,
She knows the strength in you.

She speaks.
Her quiet wisdom,
Her words may leave you numb.
She tells you to absolve you.
She sees now, what will come,

Her End
Death is not your fault my friend,
We cannot fight the odds.
You must not always blame yourself,
Death comes from the Gods.

Murdered.
Killed by one whose ignorance,
Would not let him forgive,
Whose eyes only saw savages,
Who would not let him live.

The Gift
Her hair was whiter than the snow,
The blood still stained the cloth,
His vengeance on the pure of soul
Had vented out his wrath.

The Fire
You sent her out with reverence,
Released now to the wind,
Her people will avenge her soul,
Fire will be the end.

Leaky Roof

It could wait 'til morning,
We could just move the bed,
The icy drip of water landed,
Where he laid his head.

He rose up to investigate,
Searching in the dark,
For signs of water ingress,
Where damp had made a mark,

Tools in hand and ready,
Like a soldier off to war,
Having done reconnaissance,
He's headed for the door,

Hold it soldier, freeze right there,
That's your best wool shirt,
Don't you dare go out to work in that,
You'll ruin it with dirt.

So completely naked
He climbed up on the roof.
Expression of a martyr,
As if I needed proof.

Loud dramatic hammering,
A point is neatly made,
Then freezing cold He climbs back in
The warm bed where I stayed.

Crisis thus averted,
Manly duties done,
The carpenter goes back to sleep,
Cold hands, on my bum.

Otter Tooth

A skull half buried in the leaves.
An Opal, sparkling bright,
Ghostly footprints through the mud,
The guide that set me right.

Lightning dancing in the trees,
a pole of fire burns
A rearing horse, I hit the ground.
Unconscious in the ferns

Shelter found under a tree,
I emptied out my boots,
Then made a place to lay my head,
Nestled in its roots.

Hard as rock beneath the leaves,
A skull of bleached white bone,
An opal, large to fill your hand,
The brightest coloured stone.

A torchlight waving in the trees,
Not held by mortal hand,
A ghostly silent Indian
Wandered on this land.

A ghoulish wound upon his head,
His skull was cleaved in two,
Twas clear he had a violent end,
Who was he? I'd no clue.

At dawn I found my boots had gone
Was this ghost a thief,
Then I saw the footprints,
I must follow them, relief.

I tracked them through the woodland,
I walked as in a dream,
To Jamie and the horses,
And my boots beside the stream.

The Indian spirit guided me,
But what I found most chilling,
His teeth had modern dental work,
And several silver fillings.

A sign indeed, he brought us here,
We need no longer roam,
The stream led us to Frasers Ridge,
The place we made our home.

A trip into town Summer 1768

Mrs Silversmith

I'm lookin' for the silversmith.
Say lass is he by?
Nae but ye can stay and wait,
And would ye like some pie?

How long is he gone from home?
I have nae time tae bide,
I'm happy waitin' on the door.
I will nae step inside,

He'll not be home for several days,
I fear your wait is long,
I'm a good cook and I've plenty,
And going for a song!

I'll take my leave, and business.
Forbye, I have a wife,
If I sampled what yer cooking,
I'd be paying wi my life,

I have a bonnie cook at home,
I will nae have her vexed,
Good day tae ye Mrs Silversmith
I'll try the Blacksmith next!

Murtagh – ye old Coot

The Scots are canny with their coin,
We've heard it much in verse,
A tired man, a long day's work,
I'm closed – we hear him curse!

The forge was killed, His hammer quiet,
His tools were on the bar,
A wee Scots voice implored him,
We have tae travel far!

A swift negotiation,
a master robs a boy,
A purse of coin to mend a bit,
From this there'd be no joy.

Dander up, and angry,
He finds the blacksmith in!
Set to get some money back,
No man will fleece his kin.

A voice not heard for many years,
The blacksmith turns – so slow,
All those extra shillings,
Were fate, I think we know.

Four eyes filled with tears of joy,
Murtagh has been found,
The tight old coot has found his kin,
Now he must buy a round!

Fifteen extra shillings,
Was little price to pay,
Aghousti, I have missed ye so,
Will ye not come to stay.

Cut from Ellen's candlestick.
A silver ring is made,
Forged with love and Latin,
For his skill he was not paid!

Life has built a fence between.
Two men joined by a vow,
The landlord and the taxpayer,
should be opponent's now!

Beers drunk with Murtagh,
They seek to build a bridge,
Returning home, he will find Claire.
And chaos on the ridge!!

Murtagh – my godfather

He's always been there with me.
Since I lost my mother
Looked out for me and watched my back.
A mentor like no other

Sworn to give his life for mine
His loyalty unswerving.
I know that he can read my mind.
In a way which is unnerving.

Murtagh Fitzgibbons Fraser
Is part of my blood?
And I will keep an eye on him.
When no others think I should.

Tis only right that I should protect.
The one who protects me.
As long as I have air to breathe.
That is how it will be.

But he is a man who will go his way.
Until my time of need.
And when our path diverges
I wish him God speed.

For I am grown and my life now
Has different needs to his?
But he always has a place in me.
And I a place in his.

I hope I never see him waste his life.
On another pointless cause
Fighting for what he believes is right.
He is too old for wars.

When at last, I have a home.
And Claire is by my side.
I pray Murtagh stands before my fire.
Warming his backside.

Indecent Exposure

Thrown from my horse, I lay there.
In pain that made me groan
No one around to hear me,
I could die out here alone.

Lost out in the wilderness,
Unconscious, freezing cold,
Shivering, and muddy,
Exposure taking hold.

Shoes found on the threshold,
Left there by a ghost,
Taken back to safety,
To those I love the most.

Boil the water, Stoke the fire,
Bath before I sleep, serene.
I'll not be washing filthy sheets,
If I can sleep, there clean.

Shampoo, soap, hot water,
Whisky for inside,
Muddy clothes abandoned,
Along with female pride.

Tenderly he washed my hair.
Cleaned off all the dirt,
Examining my bruises,
Gentle where it hurt.

Aye she's handy with the goose grease.
When I have a chill,
Time, I tested it on her,
I will nae have her ill.

I shall get my own back,
I can'nae let this pass,
Fair is fair - this ointment stinks,
Just like the devil's arse!

The pungent smell of camphor,
Rising from my chest,
It's a thorough application,
Now - He's covering the rest.

Not just for my welfare,
My senses working loose,
The gander's getting saucy.
With a very greasy goose.

The 9th Earl – Willie

BANG!!
Is the first sound I remember.
And then silence seemed so long.
I was not frightened by the sound.
Someone kept me strong.

My parents died when I was born.
My family was fractured.
Grand pa, Grandma, my aunt, Lord John.
A family – manufactured.

And always in the background
When I was really small
Was Mac the groom,
So quiet, and calm, and strong, and really tall.

Mac taught me things, he told me NO
Without being admonished
Firm and kind and always fair
But in fear of being punished.

I learned to ride – Mac taught me well.
I learned respect for horses.
Til I was six was always there
But drawn by other forces.

When I was six, he broke my heart.
I saw him ride away.
He christened me James my papist name.
Before he left that day.

Years went by – and I grew up.
But I never forgot.
And when we met on Frasers Ridge
It went through me like a shot.

This man my papa John calls friend.
Plays chess with and admires.
I'm sure that he is Mac the groom.
Why does he not recognise me?

He did not look back that awful morn.
He caused me so much pain.
I asked him why?
He thought that we would never meet again.

A papist name, a rosary
Were all he had to give?
I won't tell him, but I treasure them.
As long as I shall live.

And wee Faith is not forgotten.
Though I always carry blame
Did my headstrong selfishness.
Put you in a grave.

And Willie, 9th Earl Ellesmere
You may deny your sire.
Look in the mirror and you'll find.
All that Fraser fire.

Lallybroch June 1769

A Lass comes riding.

So, he's back, don't lie to me!
Seen riding in the Glen,
He is not in the colonies,
Will I get my money then?

Her face was red with anger,
Tears of rage had flowed,
Laoghaire came to Lallybroch,
To claim what she was owed.

A lassie wearing breeches,
Searching for her kin,
Tall and lean with bright red hair,
A Fraser to her skin.

Welcomed by the family,
Brought into the fold,
Jamie has a daughter,
More precious here than gold.

The shrew like voice grew louder,
Wheedled and complained,
Demanded explanation,
Claiming she was shamed!

I'll know who is yer mother,
He did not treat me fair,
It takes a fire to kill a witch,
And she was always there!

I pulled myself to my full height,
My Fraser blood was riled,
I am Jamie Fraser's daughter,
Yes, and I'm Claire's child.

She very near exploded,
She called my mother bitch,
A stream of foul expletives,
Ending up with Witch!

Proof was in my pocket,
His mother's wedding gift,
Milk white pearls, a chain of gold.
She mocked them with short shrift.

Hers by right she claimed them,
Claimed she was his wife,
I told them straight, how this foul thing,
Had tried to take Claire's life.

She mumbled on decrying him,
And how he did her wrong,
How he never wanted her,
Claire's love was too strong.

A quiet manic mantra,
Jamie in her arms,
Stolen by the English witch,
Captured by her charms,

Her fetch was in their wedding bed,
He cried for her at night,
She was not dead; a witch must burn.
She knew that she was right.

A quite voice beside me,
Calming, soft and kind,
Ian Told me Claire was safe,
Like he read my mind.

She found him then! My heart leapt.
She wasn't on her own.
Reunited with her love,
Through that ring of stone.

They welcome me as one of them,
I'm loved for who I am,
I know they love my father,
He's a good and honest man.

I will travel to them,
far across the sea,
Warn them of a fatal fire.
This is my destiny.

Lizzie

Travelling to the colonies,
I didn't need a maid,
I was waiting on the dockside,
With my passage paid,

Her father owed some money,
Said another man would fetch her.
He'd rather her across the world,
Than indentured to a lecher.

So, there's me and Lizzie now,
Travelling cross the sea.
It's more me looking after her,
Than her looking after me.

Lizzie is a simple soul,
She's not seen much of life,
She's handy with the sewing,
But useless with a knife.

She likes to feel needed,
Tries hard to get things done,
But Lizzie Wemyss is terrified,
Life experience – she has none.

She's like a wounded puppy,
She follows me around,
Sometimes I'd like some kind of space.
Where I just can't be found.

And then there's her bad habit,
Of jumping to conclusions,
She thinks the worst of everything,
This sometimes means confusion.

Like, she said Roger raped me.
She told that to my Da!
Jamie beat him senseless,
The Indians took him far!

But Lizzie is forgiven now,
She had my best at heart.
She loves this mixed-up family.
Of which she is a part

A Fish out of Water

An Amazonian woman
With a mass of ginger hair,
A smile like potted sunshine
And a very blue-eyed stare.
Stood upon my doorstep.
I fell in love right there.

An old-fashioned history professor
Who sings and plays guitar,
I'm sure this six-foot angel.
Is out of my league by far.

If I could see my future,
would my life include,
A journey through the veil of time.
To a place where life was crude.

I cannot make a shelter.
I'm a crap shot with a gun.
In the Carolina back woods
Life wouldn't be much fun.

But I would follow my Brianna.
Through the mist of time.
To be half killed by her father.
For a crime that wasn't mine.

Her father would involve me.
In minor feuds and wars,
A random swarm of locusts
And helping him hang doors.

I got stuck at Alamance.
The wrong side of the beck
Lucky me – I survived.
When they hanged me by the neck.

I came good with Jamie.
When he was bitten by a snake
I refused to let him die.
He pulled through for goodness's sake.

I came to love the Frasers,
To call the ridge my home,
A big extended family
I never knew my own.

The fact that I can travel,
Is really quite a bitch,
Turns out I'm the offspring.
Of the war chief and the witch.

We tried it just the one time.
To come back through the stones
But they wouldn't send us anywhere.
When we thought of home.

We ended where we started.
The place we thought as home.
A place of peace and drama
Of violence and calm.

The place to bring up children.
Without a modern fridge
I expect Bree can invent one.
Up on Frasers Ridge.

Wilmington September 1769

Two sorts of Theatre in one

Wilmington is buzzing.
It's the hub of polite society.
But it still has a dark side.
And loads of impropriety.

The Frasers are about in town.
Going to the Theatre
Tucking in a hernia
Thrills the public better.

And while all this is going on
Roger gets to town.
Surprises Young Brianna
Makes dopey Lizzie frown.

Bree and Roger quarrel
Bree sends him away.
But he's tied to Bonnets crew.
Bonnet won't let him stay.

And Bree gets raped by Bonnet.
Tries to buy Claire's ring.
Lizzie thinks that it was Roger.
Though she didn't see a thing.

But the morning after
Lizzie nails it down
It's she who finds the Frasers.
Haven't yet left the town.

If you had to meet the father
You hadn't met at all.
Would you really like to meet him?
Pissing up against a wall!

The Family is United
They start the journey home.
But what of poor old Roger
Still working his fingers to the bone.

Quick domestic update
I'm out of Sassenach.
There's some cheap stuff in the cupboard.
Hiding at the back.

I've researched my family history.
Are there Scots? The answers yes.
My great uncle married a McGregor.
They came from Inverness.

My ever-loving husband
Has begun to decorate.
He's stuck my Jamie to the ceiling.
And I've ordered Tartan paint.

Back at the ridge
Claire has sussed Brianna is not right,
She not just missing Roger.
She cannot sleep at night.

But ever resourceful Roger,
Has made his own way back.
But Lizzie sees him coming.
Half way up the track.

You stupid thing if you're not sure.
You really didn't ought to.
Tell a man like Jamie Fraser.
That's the man that raped your daughter!

There was no interrogation.
No chance to explain.
A battle-hardened iron fist.
Can inflict so much pain.

Ian took him off the ridge.
And before he had time to talk
Roger had been sold a slave.
To a branch of the Mohawk.

That's enough excitement.
It's time to take a break.
Then we'll go and look for Roger
And put right the mistake.

A Verra Good Distraction.

The Theatre in Wilmington,
Is where we can be found,
A night out in society,
Opportunities abound,

Well, ye know I've read the classics,
They are not strange to me,
But the play they are enacting,
Is not my cup of tea.

And Tryon has informed me.
That he sent his men
To trap the regulators,
That's Murtagh's gang ye ken.

I really need to warn him,
But I'm stuck in here,
I need a big distraction,
Make sure the coast is clear.

Good fortune has me seated,
Next to Edmond Fanning,
So, I poke him in his hernia,
That didn't take much planning.

Fanning needs a doctor quick,
Or he's like to die.
Claire's will need her scalpels.
I went, quickly I won't lie.

Hitched a ride with Washington.
My Alibi in place
Sent Fergus to tell Murtagh,
Not to show his face.

Back to the Theatre,
Claire still in her gown,
Tryon and some big strong men,
Holding Fanning down.

His physician turns up to the show,
Or should we say this farce,
To cure Fanning's hernia,
Puff smokes up his arse,

But Granny has her scalpel out,
And is sticking to her cause,
She fixes Fanning's hernia.
To tumultuous applause.

Murtagh has escaped again,
And here's the funny thing.
Tryon was so distracted,
He did not suspect a thing.

I'd better have another dram.
Do not hear me wrong.
You lot better go to bed.
Morning won't be long.

Yer Granny, she will scold me.
You'll all be late for school,
She'll tak her scalpel to my bits
If yer don't obey her rules.

finding my father

The journey has been long and hard.
Last night I went to hell.
I was livid with my Roger.
I told him to go as well.

I saw my mother's iron ring.
On that Irish bastard's hand
I knew that I must get it back.
It was Jamie's wedding band.

He wouldn't take it's worth in gold.
How was I so blind?
He assaulted me and raped me.
He said payment was 'in kind.'

Next day when Lizzie woke me.
I ran down to the dock.
But Rogers boat had sailed away.
Leaving me in shock.

Here comes Lizzie running now.
Excited – in a flap.
I'm not in the mood for this.
Lizzie – cut the crap.

I've spoken to a man she says.
A man who knows the score
A woman healed a man with surgery.
At the play last night – there's more.

Her husband is called Fraser.
He's down there by the store.
Oh my god it's got to be.
My parents, I am sure.

I go down to the saloon.
I'm directed round the back.
There's a big man with a pony tail.
Standing down the track.

He's standing with his back to me.
He's well over six feet tall.
Broad shouldered and with bright red hair
Pissing up against the wall.

He senses me behind him.
Looks back in surprise.
It's like looking in the mirror.
God, I have his eyes.

His look is all suspicion.
He thinks I am a whore.
He tells me he is married.
Well, I knew that before.

He's finished what he's doing.
And turns to walk away.
'You are Jamie Fraser –
I hesitantly say.

My name is Brianna, I'm your daughter.
Comes out next.
He pulls up sharp.
His next breath whistles through his chest

His sharp blue eyes were filled with tears.
He shook and then gave a sigh.
I guess it was the first time.
I saw my father cry.

A Disturbance

In my dreams I'd seen her,
And in photographs from Claire,
I knew the profile of her face,
The colour of her hair,

Lost to me across the time,
But safe, in times of peace,
All that will be left of me,
When death brings my release.

I see her always as a bairn.
But one I never nursed,
I've nieces and I've nephews,
Seen them grow, my own life cursed.

I've felt her closer lately,
Since we've been at the ridge,
Some sense that she is with me,
Has somehow built a bridge!

No peace for the wicked,
I hear a woman's call,
Can a man not have some peace,
To piss against the wall!

There's something in the tone of voice,
Makes me turn my head,
I am the man she's seeking,
I'll no take her to my bed!

I've coin that I can give her,
If she's needin' food,
But no, she is insistent,
Without being rude.

You are Jamie Fraser?
I am, and I'm confused,
She's tall, her eyes are darkest blue,
Like sky with thunder bruised,

Long red hair, hangs down her back,
My senses start to quiver,
I'm looking in the mirror,
The dawning makes me shiver,

It's Brianna, it's my daughter,
I cannot see my way for tears,
The child I thought was lost to me,
For two hundred years.

Hunting Bees

Ye ken I did'na meet yer ma.
And who she'd grown to be,
Yer Granny left her in her time,
Twas safer there, ye see.

She came to warn us through the stones.
Of something that she'd found,
The house we'd built on Frasers Ridge,
Would burn down to the ground.

The paper said, we both were dead,
Yer Granny Claire and me,
You couldn't read the printed date.
When 'twas supposed to be.

I had to get to know her,
So, we went hunting bees,
Find out more about her,
Underneath the trees.

When your hunting bees ye ken,
First you find their flowers,
Ye follow them, through the woods,
Keep watch on them for hours.

Quietly you find a tree,
Where they made their home,
Ye see they all live in one place,
And then go out to roam.

When you find their hiding place.
You wait until it's dark,
For that's when all the bees are home.
And you can find yer mark.

Puff a bit o' smoke in,
Makes them go tae sleep.
Then you put them in yer bag,
The whole swarm ye keep.

When they wake in the morning,
They are in a different place,
And you have honey for yer bread,
Or smeared across yer face.

Yer mother's good at hunting,
She's a crack shot too ye see,
Ye din'nae mess with yer mother,
The disturbance we called Bree.

It's late now, ye'll be getting cold.
Best you get off up to bed,
Dream of honey, on yer toast
Or upon yer bread.

Go quietly, ma will tuck you in.
No - I'm not making a joke,
If you lot don't go off to sleep,
I'll be up there puffing smoke!

Not your Fault

Da, did you kill Jack Randall?
The question left my lips,
I saw him flinch at just the name,
His hands upon his hips,

The scar that marked inside his thigh,
A gruesome souvenir,
He told me of Culloden,
Did I really want to hear?

He did not remember.
who he killed or how.
But Jack Randall's bloody corpse
Lay on top of him somehow.

Did it make it better?
The fact that he was dead,
Did it silence for all time?
The turmoil in his head?

I told her that in time it fades,
The pain gets less each day,
Now it does not matter,
But it has nae gone away.

She believes it all her fault,
Was there more she could have done.
The rapist who got her with child,
Could she have fought and won.

My words do not convince her.
My next, would hurt me more,
I did my best tae anger her.
I called my daughter whore!

She slapped me hard,
I fought her, I fought her as a man,
With ease of strength of muscle,
I worked her through my plan.

I showed her how, despite her grit.
And her will to win,
She would be overpowered,
At first, she won't give in.

She kicks and bites and struggles,
It cuts me to the bone,
To hear my daughter pleading,
Da! Please stop! I'm done.

Ye could not fight him daughter,
He'd have killed you if ye'd tried,
Don't blame yourself forever,
Time will heal the hurt inside.

Then I walked in darkness,
Prayed my demons gone.
Forgave again Jack Randall
For all that he had done.

The Lord says vengeance is all his,
His sentiment is fine,
Sorry Lord, but in this case,
Bree's vengeance will be mine!

Intervention

Some bright spark suggested it.
A proposal soon was made,
Young Ian dressed up in his best,
His hair with bear grease laid.

The answer was emphatic,
The argument began.
Fraser versus Fraser,
Woman versus Man

He criticised her morals,
Her knowledge of the time,
The finger pointing gossips,
That unwed is a crime.

The child would be a bastard,
Best ye stop and think,
He'd live his life with stigma,
Would ye no wipe out that stink.

He listed men he'd thought of,
He'd tried to find a match,
But none he ken't were suitable,
His daughter was a catch.

Ian has a tract of land,
And he'll inherit mine
Marry him I'm tellin' ye,
All will then be fine.

They stormed off to the stables,
Two ginger cats at war,
All flashing eyes and waving tails.
I'd seen it all before.

Nose to nose they argued,
She would not give an inch,
The spitting and the hissing
Would make a tiger flinch.

Auntie leave them to it,
Best not intervene,
Two Frasers with the dander up
Are something tae be seen.

Once they've traded insults
And let out all the steam.
One will come out victor.
The cat that got the cream

He rode off down the mountain.
She stormed out of the house.
Making growling noises
Like a cat plays with a mouse.

He'd cursed her in the Gaelic!
I knew it was obscene,
I'm not answering her question.
What does Nighean da Ghallah mean?

They'll both return for supper,
For apologies and eggs,
They may diffuse by bedtime,
But a Fraser never begs!

Termination

An inventory of poisons,
Take note of those that kill.
Should I as a mother,
Offer her my skill.

Or other intervention,
My blades are whetted well,
Either way could kill her,
And the child as well.

In the slums of Paris
The Angel Makers wept.
Poor unwanted unloved souls,
Smothered as they slept.

Bree does not belong here,
She wants to travel back,
The child is one more burden.
That makes her outlook black,

Yet again he reads my face,
He knows what's in my mind,
Rigid now with anger,
It makes his logic blind.

Life to him is all life,
the child is of his blood.
He cannot countenance the act.
His words come in a flood.

To him it doesn't matter
How it came to be,
The child is flesh, his bone, his kin.
He does not think of Bree!

Can he not see her trauma?
She cannot escape,
The thing that grows inside her
The product of a rape.

It's not a thing I've done before,
I'm sworn to protect life,
Instinctively he knows this,
The man can read his wife.

Him desperate for a grandchild,
Does the mother have no voice,
When all is said, and anger done.
It is Brianna's choice.

Mistaken identity

Hush yer noise, sit down quiet,
I think I'll have a dram,
Rest my bones before the fire,
Shout up for yer mam.

Tonight, ye Da is in the chair.
A story he must tell,
A journey with the Mohawk,
That did'na end up well,

Tell it Well now Roger Mac,
Ye've an audience in awe
Maybe leaving out the bit,
Where I broke yer jaw!

Yer ma Bree was a headstrong Lass,
She left me in the mire,
She travelled off to find her Ma and Da
And warn them of a fire,

I followed her and found her,
We quarrelled and I left,
I couldn't bear to sail away,
My heart was broke – bereft.

So, I walked to Frasers ridge,
To find my handfast wife,
Yer Grand Da wasn't happy,
He nearly took my life.

Then yer uncle Ian,
sold me to a tribe,
a gang of passing Mohawk
I think they took a bribe,

They made me walk a long way north,
Tied up as a slave,
There was no way I could escape,
I'd just as well behave.

My Indian name was Dog Face,
Because of my great beard,
Indians do not have such things,
I think they thought it weird.

Yer Ma – she made them rescue me,
Yer Grand Da brought me back,
Yer Uncle Ian was the price,
Man for a man the craic!

Confusion in identity,
They thought me Stephen Bonnet,
A robber and a bad man,
I'm just Roger and I'm honest!

I got the chance to punch him back.
That fiend you call Grand Da,
His heid is like an iron pot,
I didn't punch him far.

But that was all in time gone by,
We're family, and kin,
The wounds are healed over,
I have forgiven him.

Now you band of heathens,
Before ye go tae bed,
Take one lesson up those stairs,
Hold it in yer heid.

Ye Da was a professor,
in another time
Evidence and research
My tools to fight a crime.

Think before your actions.
Make sure you've got the facts,
Don't go jumping in feet first,
Tis fools that do those acts.

Before you draw yer sword or dirk,
Before you throw your punches,
Make sure you've found the right boy,
Who was pulling Mandy's bunches.

Now go to bed and quickly,
The time is getting late,
Me and Grand Da need a dram,
Just to wipe the slate!

I expect your Granny's listening,
For the glasses clink,
Her broomstick's in the kitchen,
She'll be here in a wink.

Less of that now Roger Mac,
Do I have to tell you twice,
Or I shall tell the story.
Of the time you lads got lice!!

Rescuing Roger

Sassenachs are ye out there,
Come sit and make me smile,
We have na drunk a dram or two.
Together for a while.

Do ye remember Frasers Ridge
Before the land was tamed
When Roger came to look for Bree,
I still feel quite ashamed.

We knew nought of Bonnet,
And her trying to buy your ring,
Only that she'd been attacked,
Well, raped – an that did sting.

No one knew the whole of it,
I didn't know the truth.
And Lizzie acted for the best,
Accounting for her youth,

Angry does nae cover it,
My temper was a villain.
And when I came across the man,
Twas in my mind to kill him.

I din 'a need a weapon,
I've one with either fist
I did'na wait for answers,
Lost in a red mist.

Half alive and sold as slave.
A spring lamb to the slaughter
When at last the truth came out,
I nearly lost my daughter.

And so began the long trek north,
To track the Indian traders,
To bargain for our Roger Mac,
Not get mistook for raiders.

The Mohawk are not stupid,
They know the worth of men,
They adopt some folk into their tribe,
The useful ones ye ken.

The stone you carried angered them,
It came from one who travelled,
Who tried to warn of white man's ways,
Their life to be unravelled.

Roger would replace a brave,
He had survived the walk.
Hundreds of miles, behind a horse.
He could hardly talk.

I'd ha stayed there Sassenach,
To heal things with my daughter,
I did'na ken what Ian said,
When he made the deal for Roger.

He'd learned the Indian customs,
Myers had filled his heid
And now he was to stay with them,
Ach, his mother' d see me dead.

But Ian is the man he is,
Because he made that break,
Buckskins and a tomahawk,
A man of honour make,

Roger came back to the fold,
And I was soon forgiven,
Then Ian and his dog returned,
Life was again worth living.

Do ye think the weans now,
Will come to understand,
They need to see the whole of things.
Before they raise a hand.

Their Grand Da, was impulsive,
Some will say still is,
Acting without thinking,
Is a trait of his.

What do you think Sassenach,
Will they get it right,
Pick their battles carefully,
And know which ones to fight.

I need tae take ye Sassenach,
We're a bit old fer the floor,
Let me take ye up to bed.
And maybe bolt the door!

Father Ferigault

He could not see his faith that way.
He only saw Gods wrath.
Not just the doctrine of the church,
The dogma of the cloth

Sin had tainted holy vows,
Made him fall from grace,
To fall in love and sire a child,
Had turned him from Gods face.

He would not lie and bless the child.
Abuse the sacrament.
To damn his child's eternal soul
he would know what was meant.

He could have stopped the torture.
He had nothing to gain,
The racking screams the stench of flesh
The never-ending pain,

Baptise the child, Tis only words,
Don't let this be your hell.
It's all they want; you are of faith.
No matter if you fell,

All seeing lord forgive this man,
Who'd burn upon a pyre,
Take his screams up with his pain,
His faith we must admire,

They would not know the difference,
He could have been kept whole,
he knew he had betrayed his faith,
And his immortal soul,

Foolish father Ferigault,
Or one we should admire,
To make the final sacrifice
And burn in deathly fire.

Warlike men who live by blood,
Will not give you release.
Slowly they will turn the screw,
Your pain will never cease.

That one belief should come to this.
Barbaric, tortured death
His faith so strong, all pain defied.
A scream his final breath.

They lit the fire beneath his feet,
Slowly stoked the flame,
Creeping heat would sear his flesh,
And then his body claim

Think of yourself, of number one,
I fled into the trees,
Escape was mine, but pain was his
It brought me to my knees.

I walked and thought, I heard his screams,
I argued with myself,
He made his choice, and he chose death.
Why then should I help,

Had I lost humanity,
could I not speed his way,
The Mohawk watched inscrutable.
As life was burned away.

A cask of whisky, lay at hand,
At least I'd speed his slaughter,
Pillar of fire lit up the sky,
Exploding fire water.

She placed the baby on the ground.
And walked into the flame,
Their bodies moulded in that heat.
Together in his shame.

Man for man.

So, Dog Face is worth pots and pans.
Trade trinkets for a man
Scorn dripped from the Mohawk Chief
This was not in our plan.

You value him so little.
You buy him with some beads.
He is strong, we keep him.
He works, he suits our needs.

What then is a fair exchange,
How do we buy a life.
Not with goods and chattels
Or even with a knife

Man for Man the bargain.
To live here as a slave
One of us must stay here,
Perhaps unto the grave.

I can'nae let ye do it.
I know you'd give yer life,
I will not let ye stay here.
My aunty is yer wife.

Uncle I will talk with them.
I speak their language best,
I can make a bargain.
I din'nae speak in jest.

And so, I ran the gauntlet,
They took me as a brave,
Tattooed face and buckskins
My hair a Mohawk shave.

I learned their ways; I took a wife.
I loved my Mohawk Bride
I lived the Mohawk way of life.
With Rollo by my side.

Sadness came with children lost,
When Emily the mother,
Cast me out upon the breeze,
Said goodbye to Wolfs Brother,

Home is where you go to
And they have ta take ye in,
So here I am, but what am I?
Mohawk with Scottish kin

My Worn-out Warrior.

My warrior is a raconteur,
He loves to tell a story.
He does not spare the detail.
The results can be quite gory,

He tells them all our history.
Sitting round the fire,
He's even shown them all the scars,
Not something to admire,

Their Grand da is their hero.
They treasure every word,
But if he thinks they'll get to sleep
He really is absurd,

The boys are fighting battles.
Sword and dirk in hand,
The girls are fighting with them.
They're all in Grand Da's Clan.

So, I'll leave the warring clansmen.
Until it's time for bed,
I'll listen to his stories.
While I bake the bread.

He could sit there for hours,
Weans wrapped up in his plaid.
Enthralling them with stories,
Of the wondrous times he's had.

Rapt In sheer amazement,
He teaches them the names,
Of Clansmen fighting Redcoats,
Painting pictures in the flames.

I sometimes sit beside him,
Head upon his knee,
And wonder if he's told them.
Of the day that he met me.

Tonight, I'm only fit for bed,
I won't interrupt his flow,
He's getting to a good bit,
I can feel the tension grow,

They'll ask for one more story,
Before they go to bed,
Then my worn-out warrior
May come and rest his head.

Less of the Worn out! Sassenach,
As up the stairs you creep,
I've not lost all my faculties.
To bed now! – not to sleep.

The Grimoire and the Ghost.

A battered notebook bound in green.
Abandoned at that site.
Its owner gone into the past,
And murder done that night,

Research aye and ravings
The theory of a loon,
Committed here to paper,
No familiar or broom

'It is a witches name I take,
No matter of my own,
I seek only the power of flesh,
But surrender not my bone.

Death is for surrendered souls,
I seek power absolute,
I find it makes the mind corrupt,
While I am more astute.

I study those who tried before,
No sacrifice they send.
Bodies weakened by the force,
They meet a grisly end.

Samhain is the first of feasts,
When souls of heroes rise,
Those born when the stars aligned.
Have power as their prize.

Few will find the courage.
To use that gifted night
To leave the grave and walk abroad,
To seek what is their right.

To build an image from the stars
To walk where few would tread.
To live a life that lies between
The living and the dead.

There will be one, so prophesied.
His true life yet to be,
His power incorruptible
Will help to set us free.

He seeks one who will travel.
A soul brave as his own,
One born of the auld ones.
With power of her own.

And if we fail as history says,
As prophesied by seers,
The child born of this true line,
Will cross two hundred years.

Regulators

Taxes are the curse of life.
Yet they must be paid,
Used to run the Government,
And the money not waylaid.

Collected up by honest men.
Who only take what's due?
And not diverted to the pockets
Of the corrupt and powerful few.

But the rich who run the Country
Are greedy to the core.
Will take the food from honest men.
And then they ask for more.

Dishonest men all on the take
Collect the revenue,
They levy more than a man can make.
And then they add their due.

A lot of us were sent here,
As punishment ye ken.
And now we have our freedom back.
We won't be chained again.

Don't boast about your mansion.
Fit to host the King and Queen
Built with our tax money.
Your morals are obscene.

We will band together.
And fight for tax that's fair.
You may not see it coming.
But a war is in the air.

The Gathering of October 1770

The Butter churn.

Father Kenneth was arrested.
And under some portent
Desirous of his services,
We stole into the tent.

To get his grandson christened
Jamie must distract the crowd.
So, he made confession.
Embarrassingly loud

His lewd imagination
Had run amok it seems,
With a lassie churning butter,
Who stirred alluring dreams.

He watched her at the handle.
The rhythm stirred his lust.
Breasts heaving with the motion,
Pull and push and thrust,

Her skirts swayed to the movement.
Her face aglow with sweat
Impure thoughts ran through his mind.
And through his body swept,

He saw her pitching forwards,
Bent across the churn,
Skirts hitched high above her waist,
His ardour starts to burn,

And I outside the tent flap,
Speechless and amazed
Listened as he outlined.
His intentions – quite depraved!

Described in every detail,
Every squeak she'd utter,
And everything he'd done to turn.
Her insides into butter!

I remember that encounter well,
My cheeks begin to burn,
Remembering the afternoon
We broke the butter churn!

My Daughter's Wedding

I've only known her lately,
Now I'm giving her away,
My wee girl getting married,
Today her wedding day.

Old the pearls around her neck,
New, whisky from the still
Borrowed, is my time with her,
Blue, the flowers, from the hill.

The groom is waiting, nervous.
He's nearly cut his throat,
I had tae help him shaving,
He's blood all down his coat.

The Frasers of the Ridge are here,
To celebrate this match,
And the Governor and his redcoats,
With politics to hatch.

A Presbyterian service,
No Latin and no Priest,
Ye ken they are all heretics!
But they're married now at least.

With my brown-haired lass beside me
We remember all our vows,
From this day forth, and until death,
Are all that God allows.

One man sorely missing,
There's no Murtagh at this do,
But the Bride has sixpence from him.
Tucked inside her shoe.

I sense a presence watching,
A spirit from the dead,
Watching from the shadows
Frank will see MY daughter wed.

There's music and there's dancing.
They'll drink until they fall,
You can rely on Lord John Grey,
To out drink them all.

With young Jemmy in our care,
It's off to bed we're heading,
Feuds and battles set aside,
At this family wedding.

But Jocasta is still scheming,
An heir is still her goal.
As Roger Mac so aptly said,
Cram it up yer hole!

The Call to Arms

He lit the cross, fire at his back,
Red hair gleamed in the flames,
So, Tryon says he wants a Scot,
Let's play him at his games.

A highland figure dressed in plaid,
His voice is ringing out,
Calling all to stand by him,
And all thronged to his shout,

An oath was sworn, stand by his hand,
Though they are not a Clan
Settlers all, in this new land,
They will stand by this man.

A figure framed in leaping fire,
Dirk and sword a glow
Arms spread to call his people close,
To face a common foe,

A Rally cry to all who hear,
Emotive words are spoken,
Eloquent in rhetoric
An oath not to be broken,

Inspiring all to loyalty
A community bound tight.
To stand beside its founder
And fight for what is right.

His people see the strength of him,
The steel inside the man,
Forged in the fire of forty-five,
And tempered by his land.

Horses for Courses Gideon

Sour is a perfect word.
To describe this horse,
A mean streak running through him,
He won't be tamed with force.

Bought cheaply for this reason,
A temper that's a try on,
So, sound of wind, he'll go all day,
But his mouth is hard as Iron.

He bucks and runs away with you,
He cat leaps and he rears.
So quick he'll dump you on your arse,
Or out over his ears.

Only one man rides him,
He's a bastard of a horse,
Impatient and delinquent,
The bosses mount – of course.

Threatened with castration.
But no one ever dares,
He makes the Ridge a fortune.
Serving Indian mares

Mighty man of valour,
The meaning of his name,
It takes one of those to ride him,
James Fraser knows his game!

Adso

I've been captured by a human,
A large human at that,
A big, tall one with ginger hair,
And a very funny hat,

I was lying out, up on the ridge.
Scratching by my ear.
The human stuffed me down his coat.
It's nice and warm in here.

The journey on the horse was wild,
The horse was misbehaving,
So, I crawled into his bag,
A bag that was worth saving.

I think he thought he'd dropped me,
Went back and had a look,
But I was safe inside by then,
Curled up in a nook.

I'd better introduce myself,
I climbed onto their bed,
Then he called me Adso.
'What's one of those?' I said.

I now work in the surgery.
Catching mice and rats
Everybody has a job.
Even kidnapped cats,

22nd November 1777 Tryon calls the Militia.

Warriors Prayer

Water fresh straight from the earth,
Wash the world away,
A Warrior, I should cleanse my soul,
Before I face this day,

Make peace with those who went before,
Clear my mind of troubles,
Sluice the guilt of other wars,
Absorb the springs clear bubbles.

Pray to those who in my past,
Have asked no recompense,
Those ones that build my inner wall,
My last line of defence,

I call them down, each one by one,
Pray they bring their shields,
I feel them standing with me,
Their strength says do not yield.

Father, Brother, And my right,
Spirits from my past,
And he who taught me all he knew,
Best I call him last.

Fierce and warlike Uncle,
Ye taught me how tae fight,
No quarter to be given,
Ye never saw that light.

Drawing blood will bring him near,
His lessons call to mind,
Select my enemy with care,
Or cut those ties that bind.

There is no other spirit,
I'd have at my left side,
Fight with me now, in this new fight,
Let justice be yer bride.

Ready now to face what comes,
Kiss me Sassenach,
'Take care Soldier' sends me off,
But your love brings me back.

Time and motion

Will we ever understand,
The reason for a fate?
The underlying purpose
Which makes an action great.

What you call disaster,
Was it meant that way?
Or does it bring significance?
To another day?

For we will never see the end,
The final scene and act.
The train of Time keeps rolling on,
Despite our small impact.

A day that's changed, a thing not done
It sounds like one big riddle,
Things of the past affect us now,
But we are in the middle.

The things we do will make a mark.
Somewhere in time to come,
But we may never see that time,
Death may leave us numb.

Writers of our history
See what was left behind,
The do not know the reasons why.
The truth they never find.

The hero and the villain,
The drunkard and the fool,
Songs are writ about their lives,
With music as a tool.

The dead are long since buried,
They lie beneath their stones,
If they could have seen the future,
They may have made old bones.

Is there some higher power,
Dictating how we climb?
Are we only puppets?
On the map of time?

I spilled my all to Roger,
To make him understand,
The consequence of changing things,
Interfering with fates hand,

For travellers can affect things,
By what they leave behind,
And time runs on continually,
To the end of all mankind.

Goats and Hell

Josiah told us where it was.
The cabin in the wood
It stank of goat; it stank of hell.
It stank of nothing good.

Dark and uninviting,
How could anyone survive?
In a rundown hovel in the trees.
Was anyone alive.

Ahoy the house, we called out,
Jamie held the gun.
No answer, was there no one there,
Had everybody run.

A face came to the window,
Threatening but afraid,
A woman, worn by hardship.
From the righteous path had strayed.

To buy the twins their freedom,
The reason for this call.
What was in this house of horrors,
Really capped it all.

She had tortured old man Beardsley,
Just keeping him alive,
Enough to let him feel the pain.
Of burns he could survive.

He must have been a cruel man.
Death would be a blessing,
I left that one to Jamie,
With my oath I'll not be messing.

Oh God, Mrs Beardsley,
My grin is not of mirth,
Her waters have just broken,
The woman's giving birth!!

She did not take her baby,
When she left at dead of night
She found the Twins indentures,
And was gone before the light.

Wrapped up with her Indian child,
The deeds to Beardsleys land,
Someone would find a home for her,
With inheritance, understand.

We buried old man Beardsley.
Underneath a tree,
Alongside all his other wives,
I think I counted three.

We took the rest to Brownsville,
The baby and the goat
The hungry mite, foraging.
Down the front of my old coat.

I often think of Fanny,
For that is what they called her,
When we left her there in Brownsville,
As their adopted daughter.

Brownsville

I think I need a second dram,
To tell the Brownsville tale
Of my Captain Roger Mac,
And a venture doomed to fail.

Now Brownsville is a funny place,
It's verra verra strange,
All the folk are family,
Ye Ken they're no quite sane.

Forming a militia,
I needed fighting men,
There's lots of them in Brownsville,
They're a violent lot, ye ken.

Sent off on an errand.
I sent in Roger Mac,
To recruit the Browns to fight with us,
He went off down the track.

The reception wasn't pleasant,
Lionel Brown would not give quarter,
To Isiah Morton
Who had defiled his daughter.

A thorny problem to be solved,
Lionel has but one,
To cut off our Isiah's balls,
Then shoot him with his gun.

When Claire and I rode into town
The men had all been drinking,
Pissed as crickets most of them,
What was Roger thinking.

And Roger Mac my Captain
Deep amongst this throng,
Doing what he does the best,
Giving them a song.

I was nae really all that pleased,
They'd used up all the Whisky.
The Browns were still not happy,
The atmosphere was risky.

Roger had but one plan.
And he did confess,
He got them drunk and waited,
For me to sort this mess.

Ay Rogers not a fighter,
Recruiting's not his game
But when it comes to singing songs.
He puts us all to shame.

Frasers Ridge December 1770

Explaining Christmas

Ye'd better fetch the bottle,
And if it is nae rainin'
And you can tell me all about
This thing yer mams explainin'

Ye have a tree inside the house,
Ye mean ye keep it whole!
Then ye sit around it
Like some big green totem pole?

Ye dress it up with baubles,
And a star to goes at the top.
And shiny stuff called tinsel.
And fairy lights, now stop!

Twas Hogmanay in Scotland,
In days when I was wee,
Time to feast and celebrate,
To call on family,

Ye do that too, I'm glad of that.
And do ye go tae church,
Even if yer heretic,
Ye celebrate his birth.

Christmas is the birth of Christ,
Who came to save all man,
Papists, oh and heretics,
Included in the plan.

When he was born, he was so wee,
They laid him in a manger,
Kings and shepherds came with gifts,
For a child who lived in danger.

Tell me now of this great man,
Who flies round in a sleigh,
Bringing gifts to girls and boys,
To open Christmas Day,

I dinna want him landing.
Up there on my roof,
I've only just nailed down those tiles,
They're slippery under hoof.

And climbing down the chimney?
I hope the fires dead,
Can he no land on the floor,
And use the door instead!

I hear yer mother calling,
We'd all best go and see.
It's time ye had yer supper,
Just leave some fer me.

I think I'll have another dram,
While I make my plan,
All this climbing on the roof,
Tis not fer this old man,

I think that when ye go tae sleep,
I'm good at creeping round,
Yer granny says I'm like a cat,
I din'nae make a sound.

Yer grand da's good at most things,
He'll give ye a surprise.
And if he can't find reindeer,
He may just improvise!

Christmas stockings

My ginger cat had done his rounds,
And crawled back into bed,
Cold hands find a warmer place,
His arm under my head,

Muttering in gaelic,
He says a prayer or three,
Not heard since we went to war,
Far across the sea.

Exploring hands, I sense his need,
Does he never rest,
Lips are soft and soon find mine,
His kisses are the best,

In the dawn of Christmas morn
We lie under our quilt,
The years roll back, inside this womb.
The life which time has built.

The house is rousing round us,
The children wake excited,
What has landed in the night,
Their screams of joy ignited.

Grand da, growls and pulls me tight,
A very Scottish noise,
Shall I make him call his Lord,
I know what he enjoys,

The reverie is broken,
By banging on the door
Children's voices burst with glee.
They can contain no more!

Sassenach where is my shirt,
The best one without patches,
In the closet, hanging up,
It's with the plaid it matches,

I have no stockings Sassenach,
Where have my good ones gone,
all of them have disappeared,
I've not one tae put on.

He's digging in the clothes chest,
Claire! This is nae funny,
Someone has eaten all of them,
Do socks taste good wi' honey.

Giggling outside our room,
The children being bold,
Hearing Grand Da, hunting socks,
For that they would pay gold.

Sassenach, this is nae fair,
My old ones still are sodden,
I can'nae even find the ones,
I wore last at Culloden.

What was it that ye told the bairns,
Before they went tae bed,
To hang a stocking by the fire,
For that strange old man in red!

Grand da hears ye Mandy,
And Jem outside the door,
Please go and find ma stockings,
Or I'll hang ye up for sure.

A pair of fiends, they bundled in,
And fell upon our bed,
Stockings filled with goodies,
Apples, cheese, and bread

Joyous little faces,
Watch Grand da with glee,
They're hungering for breakfast,
Grand Da, is hungering for me!!

Christmas Eve

Christmas Eve, we lay in bed,
I drifted into sleep,
Then felt him slide into the night,
Blankets in a heap.

The top drawer of our cabinet,
Is always stocked with food,
Grand da is always hungry,
And always in the mood!

He reached deep into its depths,
For Bannocks, and for cheese,
Then donned his plaid and disappeared,
What was his plan for these.

I looked out of the window,
And saw him in the snow,
Mark the ground with deer hoof tracks,
Just where a sleigh would go.

I asked him where its feet had gone,
That butchered Christmas deer
It had no hooves; they'd been cut off.
He said he'd no idea!

I heard a thump above my head.
he climbed up on the roof,
And marked a track across its ridge,
With a stolen hoof.

A glass of whisky by the fire,
A bannock and some beer
A carrot for the reindeer,
A stop for Christmas cheer.

I knew he had been making things,
And there beside his chair,
A single wooden reindeer.
For each child in our care.

And there is one included,
For one we lost, he said,
For Faith is what has brought us here,
Her reindeer's nose is red!

Catlike he returns to bed,
And draws me to his chest,
Cold hands, cold feet to steal my warmth,
His head upon my breast,

Grand Da's gifts they'll treasure.
More than any toy,
Each one carved with timeless love,
And each one filled with joy!

Christmas Morn

Snow lies heavy on The Ridge
It weighs down every bough,
Moonlight glistens in the trees,
All is asleep, for now.

One night of tranquillity,
When all things lie at peace,
All differences are put aside,
In slumbers soft release,

Soon all life will waken,
Christmas Day will dawn,
Life's hive of activity,
Will buzz loud on this morn,

Exited bairns with joyous smiles,
Will rise before their time,
Giggling and merry,
They plot their next great crime,

My arms around the one I love,
I'm warm on this braw night,
My errands done, I draw her close,
I feel the spark ignite.

Laird, leader, landlord
Father, Grand da and Himself
And just for one night of the year,
A red-haired Christmas Elf.

Lying in the darkness,
We truly have one soul,
With her I have no other form,
With her I become whole.

Breaking dawn awakes the ridge,
The crime is truly shocking,
Can ye no help me Sassenach,
The kids have pinched ma stockings!

Merry Christmas

Surprise

Wool supplied by Jenny's sheep,
Spun by Marsali's hand,
On the wheel made by Brianna,
Dyed as Lizzie planned,

Balls of yarn in many hues,
The colours of the trees,
Kept me busy through the nights,
A secret e'en from bees.

I'm not the best at klickit,
Young Ian taught me best,
Easy for a Scotsman,
They learn it at the breast!

My needles are best stitching,
Mending holes in skin,
I'm like a pig with chopsticks!
But I am not giving in.

Sticking to the pattern
That was with danger fraught,
Well, it was in Gaelic,
So, I read it as I thought.

Proud as punch I finished,
My homemade Christmas gift,
Crept up to the bedroom.
Dressed only in my shift,

My effort lies beneath the tree,
Completed before dawn,
Something special for himself,
A surprise for Christmas morn.

What are these now Sassenach?
He held them up with pride,
The tears of mirth that followed.
Would not be denied,

One was long and baggy,
Striped like candy cane,
The other much much smaller,
How could I explain!

Sassenach, they're wonderful,
He gasped between guffaws,
Put a wee flap at the back,
They could be winter drawers!

I ken they're meant as stockings,
I din'nae mean tae laugh.
Sure, one can keep my cock warm,
The other is a scarf!

Back upstairs now Sassenach,
I mean tae wear ma gift,
I can'nae wait ta get ma Christmas sock.
Right Under yer shift!

Enough

We've never had much place for 'things'
We've led a migrant life,
Home is where we lay our heads,
Or where I find my wife,

All the things we've left behind,
No matter what they cost,
She never seems to miss them,
She just accepts their loss.

If we could nae carry it,
If it was nae gold
Sentiment would play no part,
Everything was sold.

Now we have some respite,
For now, the fight has ceased.
A quiet space between the wars,
A little spot of peace.

A set of pearls, a silver ring,
All she has of me,
What then should I leave for her,
Underneath the tree.

A moments peace and quiet,
A lifetime in my arms,
My body and immortal soul
To keep her safe from harm

Devotion, yes and passion
Until we turn to dust,
Faithfulness and honesty
And just a hint of lust.

I'd love tae see her dressed in silks,
More often she's in rags,
Leather apron round her waist,
Brandishing my dags.

She's no' materialistic,
She has nae need for 'stuff.'
I'll just be me, under the tree,
And pray that is enough.

Happy New Year

Open all the windows.
Open all the doors,
Time to let the old year out,
Time to take a pause,

Raise a glass and make a toast,
This last year is no more,
Drink a dram and see her off,
A strange one to be sure.

Remember though the good times,
There will have been a few,
Every year holds memories,
Move on without ado.

Life is for the living,
Do not be downcast.
Nothing is there to be gained,
From living in the past.

Throw open all your windows,
Open up your doors,
Welcome in a fresh new year,
And start a dream that's yours.

A Dance of Swords

An omen for the outcome,
Who will win the day?
Predict the course of battle,
Before you meet the fray

A dance of strength and energy
Of nimble feet and grace,
Mind focused on the coming fight,
The enemy you face.

Blades a cross upon the floor,
The dancer must show skill,
Footwork swift, balance kept,
Unseen the foe you kill.

With Head bowed deep recalling
He stepped onto the floor,
Standing in a far-off land,
Beneath his feet a moor.

The formal bow, his fighting arm
Makes a courtly sweep.
Sure, footed as a highland stag.
My dancer starts to leap,

Back to a land of memories,
I see them in his face,
A distant sadness haunts his eyes,
Lost in time and place.

Clapping hands and stamping feet,
Mac Dubh, Mac Dubh, they roar!
He dances for the Ardsmuir men,
To appease the gods of war!

MacDuh will dance for all tonight,
A New Year we will meet,
When all will need to hear the call
And march to just one beat.

He sees the times a changing,
Will turn to face what comes,
Stepping lively to the music,
And dancing to wars drums

All Life Through a Lens

Sitting in my surgery,
I marvelled at the sight.
Held captive now for science,
They swam with all their might.

Deposited the night before,
Evidence of passion,
I'd kept them just to test the lens,
But I'd tease him in my fashion.

What are ye doing Sassenach?
He strolled into the room,
Invited then to have a look,
He peered into the gloom.

Are they no' gerrms? he queried,
Should they no have wee teeth!
I smiled and told him what they were,
Laughing underneath.

They are sperms – male seed.
In confusion then he wallowed,
How on earth did ye come by them?
Eyebrow raised, he swallowed!

You left them with me just last night,
I told him with a wink,
He put his eye back to the lens,
With a two eyed blink.

Look at the wee strivers,
They've handsome tails I see.
Quite proud of his effort
He talked of them with glee.

In the right environment
They'll live a week or so.
What do ye do then Sassenach,
When ye let them go.

Fine wee things, the seed of life,
Din'nae flush them round the bend!
When ye've finished watching them
Give them a fitting end!

Roger Mac and the plague of Locusts.

Here's one I have nae told ye,
It's all about yer da,
Wee Roger Mac – a clever man,
And my daughter - she's, yer ma!

Me and Granny were away,
Roger was in charge,
Folk would likely go to him.
With problems, small and large.

There was a buzzing in the air,
And no – it wasn't bees!
A swarm of locusts filled the sky,
Coveting the trees,

This evil little beastie
Eats with all its might,
Will ruin all your growing crops.
Right before your sight,

What could they do on Frasers Ridge,
Rogers does not farm.
But his educated thinking
Saved the ridge from harm.

To stop a swarm of insects,
Create a cloud of smoke,
Most of them will fly on by,
If they land, they'll choke.

He lined the fields with pots of shit.
Mixed it up with earth.
It burned with a disgusting smell,
And smoked for all it's worth.

I would na have known just what tae do.
But Roger earned his pay.
Creating smoke – stopped our folk,
Losing all they had that day.

Roger Mac is a professor,
But not what you expect,
The man who wed my daughter.
Had now earned my respect.

River Run March 1771

Wiley Mr Wylie

Arrogant, and foppish,
His makeup and his wig,
His over courteous manners,
Lipstick on a pig!

He thinks himself a man of style,
With words that paint him pretty,
He flatters, and insinuates,
But isn't very witty.

Women are a conquest,
A notch upon his sword,
To turn him down, unheard of.
God's gift thinks he is adored.

A dandy in his satins,
All fashion in his silks,
Walking cane, beauty spot,
The crowd he always milks.

In league with the devil,
That's how he funds his life,
And sets his cap for an affair,
With Jamie Frasers wife.

Persistent in advances,
Abhorrent to his core,
Claire may be in trouble,
He will force his case for sure.

Her ever-watchful husband,
Looking for his wife,
He knows just where to find her,
For she is his life.

There really is no contest,
In what will come to pass,
An angry Jamie Fraser
Will sit Wylie on his arse.

A short interrogation,
On threat of certain pain
A deal is done for Bonnets life,
And Claire can breathe again.

A hand of cards

Privacy so nearly gained,
The moments passion shattered,
Heat dispersed, in words so cool,
One wouldn't think I mattered!

Saving face and dignity,
I think I catch the,
He's just deferred a night with me,
For a hand of whist.

A game of skill and luck at cards,
For those who have a stake,
He'd take the last gold thing I own.
Franks ring, for goodness's sake!

We'll let him have the two of them,
Both marks of possession,
Bloody man, he'd gamble both,
To vent his damned aggression,

He wagers with part of my life,
That stake part of my soul,
He has some other purpose,
To hurt me, not his goal.

He'll ride his luck, right to the edge,
Oblivious of course,
My feelings trampled in the dirt,
And under Wylies horse!

That night I dreamed of Friesians,
Black stallions in the night,
Then the king of Ireland,
Woke me up in fright.

A hand beneath the bedclothes,
Is massaging my toe,
Curling round my instep,
It's grip not letting go.

Wandering hand in darkness,
Large and deft of touch,
Assured of destination,
The release I crave so much.

Its owner hid in shadows,
I pray my thoughts are right,
The hand that comes to claim me.
Is my Scotsman of the night?

Morning comes dishevelled,
Hungover, dressed in haste,
Waiting in the doorway
All trace of guilt erased!

A hand of cards, a fist of rings,
Did I doubt he'd win,
An eyebrow raised, a laser stare,
Just a hint of grin.

Gold for left, silver right,
Reclaimed in the stable,
As horses wake and humans stir,
We'll stand up if we're able.

The Frenchman's Gold

Gold, with three bright diamonds,
Jocasta showed the ring,
Light of many candles
made the white stones sing!

A diamond for each daughter,
And all of them now gone,
Ye ken I was a mother once,
My heart was not a stone,

Three husbands, and three daughters
All of them now dead,
The Cameron thirst for wealth the cause,
Ye should not be misled.

A daughter shot, for three gold bars.
The youngest of my fold,
Lying with the redcoats
Dead beside the road.

The Frenchman's gold is buried.
It lies in Scottish soil,
We could'na carry all of it,
With a country in turmoil.

Three bars were all we carried,
This fine estate they grew.
But tis a hollow empty thing,
With none to leave it to.

Is that the truth? I asked him,
His whispered voice abjured.
Remember she's MacKenzie blood.
Do not believe a word!

Her daughters – yes there's truth in it.
Her husband would nae wait.
He would na let her say goodbye,
They left them to their fate.

As for leaving gold behind,
That's not the Cameron way,
She's got it hidden somewhere,
Sure, as night turns into day!

Battle of Alamance, May 16th, 1771

Taking Stock

Ten toes, two feet
Two legs - that's neat
Nearly lost one of those.

Fingers – nine
But that's just fine,
If the rest work – I suppose.

Two arms to hold the one I love,
One heart – still beating- strong.

One chest – where someone's head can rest.
To check the heart has not gone wrong.

Two eyes – to see the whole of you.
Not quite so sharp this year.

Two ears – they hear you laughing.
A sound I love to hear.

One nose to hold the scent of you.
Two lips to tell you that…….

The best bit is all working fine ....
Happy Birthday Sassenach!

Nine Lives

I was told once that I have nine lives,
That nine times I would die,
Sometimes I try and count them up,
God knows why I try,

One – was when they flogged me,
The day my father died,
Two – the axe wound in my heid,
About which Dougal lied.

Three – was tortured by Black Jack,
When You brought me from the dark,
Four was on Culloden field,
Where I should have left my mark.

Five- was shot by Laoghaire, when You
Came back as my wife.
Six – a snake bite to my leg
fever nearly took That life.

If I count the shipwreck
Then I'm up to seven,
And all the times I'm shot and stabbed.
That makes about eleven.

Sassenach, I'd value.
Your professional opinion,
Which bits of me are still alive,
They're all in your dominion.

Come check out all my faculties,
I think there's still some life,
Take inventory of all my parts.
It's your duty as my wife!

Attention Soldier!

Lay your head now Soldier,
Let me ease your mind,
Rest it here upon my breast,
Some comfort you may find,

Shoulders back now Soldier,
Let me apply the oil.
Set free the trials of the day,
Distract you from your toil,

About turn! Soldier,
I run my palms all down your back,
Tracing out those ancient scars,
Hands iron out each crack.

Now rest easy Soldier,
You are safe under my hands,
Muscles torn from acts of war,
Stretch like elastic bands.

(What is one of those Sassenach?)

Is it time for action Soldier,
The parts I have not mentioned.
Have listened to my Sergeants drill,
Look you're standing to attention!

Quit yer talking Sassenach,
Come and make some squeaks.
You know, the ones I like the most,
I've not heard them for weeks,

Shall I pin ye underneath me,
When ye've oiled me some more,
Then you'll make some noises
That you've never made before!

A Coat of Red

Have you got yer nightclothes on,
Has the baby got her rattle,
Sit down now and listen hard.
We're going to a battle.

A sly man governor Tryon,
As wily as a Scot,
Always tries to get his way,
And does as like as not.

I'd raised a good militia,
And brought them to the fray,
To fight the regulators
At Alamance that day.

He knew what he was doing,
I'd rather I was dead,
Than turn out on a battlefield
In a coat of red.

He'd even got my measurements.
It was a perfect fit.
But it burned me when I put it on,
I canna get out of it.

He knows that as a Scotsman,
I won't be for the King,
To dress me in a coat of red
Is a power thing.

Designed to show the dominance.
Of England and the Crown
Humiliate our spirit,
Completely grind us down.

If I wear this coat of red
I'll stand out in the crowd,
It puts a target on my back.
Says 'shoot me' right out loud.

I'm no a verra vain man.
But as I said tae Claire,
Red is'nae ma colour,
It clashes with ma hair.

When the fight was over,
The regulators beat,
I ripped off that blood red jacket,
And threw it at his feet.

Children I was sad that day,
Enough tae make me cry,
One of my men shot Murtagh.
I saw my godfather die,

Fill my glass, I'll drink a toast.
And pour one for yer Gran.
We'll drink a toast to Murtagh!
Exasperating man

Surgeons Kit

Pass me down that leather roll,
I'll show you what's inside,
That's my surgeons travelling kit.
I pack it when we ride.

There are all the things that I might need.
When we are at war,
Grand Da won't leave me behind,
He lost me once before.

So, I travelled with the men,
When I was in my prime
I trained as a surgeon.
Before I travelled back in time.

Scalpels – make incisions.
Cutting through the skin,
Forceps – for removing things,
Better out than in.

A pot of threaded needles,
Sterilised and ready,
For stitching wounds in battle,
You need a hand that's steady.

See that precious box just there,
That contains syringes,
For injecting penicillin,
Never mind the whinges.

I've used it on your Grand Da,
When he was infected,
I've jabbed that needle in his bum,
Even if he objected.

And then there are my bone saws.
To use for amputation
And irons for the fire
For cauterisation.

I can hear ye Sassenach,
I sense your eyes are gleaming.
Mending human beings
Is the stuff that sets you dreaming.

Watch yer Granny children,
She trained up as which,
I really should' a had her burned,
Before she made one stitch.

A Ghoistidh,

Do not waver!
And he did not
The hunters shot was true,
It burned through clothing, searing flesh,
It tore a heart in two.

Dinna Fash!
And he did not
'It does'nae hurt' he said.
Fine words, from a fine brave man
I could nae see him dead.

Help Me!
So, we carried him.
Limp into the tent,
Save him, please, ye have to!
A Ghoistidh, is not spent.

Hold my words?
I did not!
I said what none would dare,
To wage war for one's own glory,
Was never to be fair.

Duty done!
I've finished,
I'll no more serve the Crown,
That coat burned on my shoulders,
I threw it on the ground.

Goodbye!
Beloved kinsman,
Guardian of my life,
Your blood is salty with my tears,
my daughters and my wife's

Am I ready!
No, I am not.
Now I face the toughest test,
Murtagh Fitzgibbons Fraser
I must lay your soul to rest.

Peaceful!
I release you,
Lay your soul to sleep,
Your spirit will protect me,
It needs no oath to keep.

Justice!
No, there was none,
For the loyal men that fell,
The musket ball that pierced your heart
Ripped mine apart as well.

Godson

Can ye keep the lad from trouble.
They'd like tae see me try.
To keep young James from straying,
That will need an extra eye,

A boy without a mother
Will surely lose his way.
No jail has bars tae hold him.
And with stripes he'll likely pay

Ginger, headstrong, wilful!
And handy with a sword,
He'll surely draw attention.
If my judgement is nae flawed

My oath is to protect him,
Serve, in hours of need.
He surely keeps me on ma toes.
Trouble follows him indeed.

His father did a fine braw job.
The lads well read, and bright
He's wasted as a soldier,
Yet he's always near a fight!

He drives me tae distraction.
He's lucky as a cat,
A skull as thick as iron pot,
Not much can lay him flat.

Be his moral compass,
Steer him t'wards a goal.
I'm no' a man who's much for God.
No prayer will save ma soul.

Sometimes I get tae thinkin,
I'm old fer prison breaking now,
I should ha read the small print,
Before I made the vow.

Dying did nae hurt at all.
I watch now from above,
My feet up at Gods table,
Just guiding him, with love

Breathe Again!

Breathe!
There's rope around my neck,
Breathe!
I am not dead.
Breathe!
A barrel at my feet
A sack over my head.

Breathe!
They did not tie my hands,
One protects my throat.
Breathe!
Please see the flag of truce
Hanging from my coat.

Breathe!
I'm hanging, kicking air.
But I'm still alive,
Breathe!
Pray God they look for me,
Then maybe I'll survive.

Breathe!
I see them through the sack,
My hold on life is weak,

Breathe!
Thank God, they've seen me,
I can no longer speak.

Breathe!
Strong arms support my weight.
The rope no longer tight
Breathe!
I hit the blessed earth.
Have I the will to fight?

Breathe again!
I am not dead,
But I am scarce alive,
Claire can give me life again.
Pray God I will survive.

Breathe!
The last thing that I saw.
Hanging from the tree,
When the rope jerked round my neck,
The face I saw was Bree!

Breathe!
I have survived the hanging tree,
My fate was Gods own choice,
He let me keep the ones I love,
But took away my voice.

Breathe!

Astrolabe

The pedlar left his donkey.
Grazing in the yard,
Handed me the parcel,
Red and breathing hard.

A box wrapped up in oilcloth,
Tied around with twine,
The seal long gone in transit,
It smelled of tar and brine.

It sat 'til after dinner.
Like an unexploded bomb,
Waiting to announce itself,
And do it with aplomb?

Wrapped in scarlet velvet.
Encased inside a box.
An instrument of beauty,
It's golden finish shocks!

Eyes live with amusement.
Amongst the puzzled crowd
What is it? Was the question.
The answer given, proud.

Tis the planispheric astrolabe,
   I ordered from Lord John
   I did'na need a gold one.
   Pewter would have done.

Ye use it for surveying,
   He handed it to Bree.
   I learned how tae use one.
      In Paris don't ye see

They examined the engraving,
   Called extravagance a crime,
Then father took his daughter out
   To learn to tell the time.

An instrument of quality,
   The engraving seems alive.
Align the discs and you will know.
   It's twenty-five past five.

He stiffened as he read the note.
   Suffice it all to say.
This instrument had not been bought.
   By his good friend Lord John Grey

I felt the arrow strike its mark.
   The barb stuck in his heart.
   William 9th Earl Ellesmere
   In this had had his part.

Buy the finest and the best,
To him this would mean gold,
A token from a lifelong friend,
And the son he could not hold.

Shadows in the Hearth

Shapes in shadows on the wall,
Reflect in tongues of fire,
Lying sated, in the warmth
Of flames and loves desire,

You are a thing of beauty,
I can'nae say too much.
Could ye say the same of me,
Do I attract yer touch,

Sassenach I'm gettin' auld,
There's white now in ma hair,
Ma beard is turning scabbit grey,
Do ye still see me fair?

I trace his features in my mind.
The scars under my hand,
We've both grown older, such is time,
And time is in command,

I see the streaks of silver,
Where copper once was bright,
But silver shines as brightly,
I'd not care if it were white,

A beauty carved of hardship,
Worn and used by life,
Moulded by adversity,
Tempered by great strife,

My eyes will see you change each day,
My hands and arms will feel,
The force of life within you,
The strength that makes me heal,

Beauty is subjective,
More than in the eye,
And you who fires my very soul,
Your beauty makes my cry.

The Knack of being married.

How do I do marrit?
I can'nae learn from books,
That message passed without a voice,
Sent in touch and looks.

He watches her intently,
Senses every move,
Her hands convey her feelings.
His eyes project his love,

The secret bonds of couples,
The sparks that make them burn
Are they born within you,
Or things that I must learn,

They dance around each other,
Desire spikes the air,
I swear he even smells her.
I see his nostrils flare!

As natural as breathing
No self-conscious blush
I fear I have disturbed them.
But for them there is no rush,

A fleeting kiss, a brush of lips
The slightest touch of hand,
A farewell and an I love you.
Her wish is his command.

How do I learn these lessons,
Can I ever replicate,
The unseen knack of marriage
Before it is too late

The Hayloft.

Do ye remember Sassenach,
When we were first together,
Finding places we could hide,
And lie upon the heather,

Like naughty bairns who skip'd off school.
We'd rush time through our chores,
Ye'd meet me in the stables,
With the deep straw of the floors,

I could nae wait tae touch ye,
Live flame in my hand,
You burned a path into my heart,
A love that was not planned.

That feeling we could not explain,
Is still as strong for me,
I can'nae lie beside ye,
And not hold ye close ye see.

Yes, I feel the pull of you,
I never need to roam.
Wherever this world takes us,
Your body is my home,

High up on the mountain,
We'd lie beneath the stars,
My hands upon your body,
I'd trace your many scars,

Familiar as a route map,
I know each silver line,
Each blade, each burn, each musket ball,
Each stitch which healed was mine,

The match which lit my inner fire,
Was kindled from your flame,
You awoke my inner self,
A thing you still can't tame,

Yes, you are my master,
For as long as I allow,
As I am yours, if you agree,
We both know the score by now,

Fetch a blanket Sassenach,
Let's find a place that's soft,
I recall we used to love,
The hay up in the loft.

Pull up the ladder from the world,
With the horses down below,
I'd make ye scream beneath me,
Dear Lord, I want ye so!

If I can get ye up there,
I shall keep ye there the night,
I'll serve ye well and make ye squeak,
We'll stay there till it's light,

Do you think we have it in us,
We might give the horse a fright,
Remember you're a grandad.
Are you up for twice a night?

We lie here in the darkness,
Each other's only thought,
A love as strong as folded steel,
On time's anvil wrought.

I hear Brianna call us,
Our laughter seems most fitting.
Tonight, she has no earthly chance,
Of Grand Da babysitting

Down wind

We tracked them through the forest,
I saw them through the trees,
A herd of beasts grazed quietly,
Ears twitching in the breeze,

Buffalo, and many,
The Ridge would have its meat,
No hungry bellies this year,
Now we must be fleet!

Ach Fergus the wee heathen,
This is nae some French farce.
He's more time with his breeks half-mast.
Than covering his arse

Get yer act together man.
Take yer men around the herd.
I'll take the back wi' Roger Mac
Then wait for my word.

Half fermented sauerkraut?
Aye that would be the cause,
Gripping in his belly
En Francais 'zut Alors!

Ach Fergus, go man, shake yerself.
The hunt about to start,
May I suggest ye stay downwind
If ye intend tae fart.

Bitten by a Snake

I didn't see it coming,
But an exploded powder keg
Of pain went through my body
As it flowed into my leg.

My eyes were on the buffalo.
It was a big mistake.
To not look all about me -
I didn't see that snake.

Its poison slowed my senses.
I felt myself go cold.
But my leg was throbbing hot as hell.
Fever taking hold.

I couldn't walk, I couldn't crawl,
Could barely raise my head.
If Roger couldn't get me home.
I'd verra soon be dead.

Roger Mac! now is the time.
To really show your worth,
Me dying in the bushes.
Is not a time for mirth.

He made me stay quite quiet.
He prayed for me a bit.
In English not in Latin
The Presbyterian twit!!

He built a sledge of branches.
And dragged me from the wood.
Until they came to look for us,
I didn't think he could.

Roger never gave an inch.
Though I was racked with pain
He cursed me and cajoled me.
As the poison coursed my veins.

Claire was clearly frightened.
She wasn't making jokes.
Her cheerful bedside manner
A nervous, see through, hoax.

So, she filled the hole with maggots,
And made me drink her broth.
She thought I couldn't see the saw.
She hid under the cloth.

I'd rather die a whole man.
Than live with half a leg
She'll not touch me with that saw.
No matter how she begs.

She could not inject me,
For lack of a syringe.
My arse was safe from needles,
Though the maggots made me cringe.

Stubborn and rebellious
I'd die a proper man.
With two whole legs, and all my bits.
At least that was the plan.

And I'd die in my own bed.
With my wife beside me.
I'm going out a happy man,
With God alone to guide me.

A determined woman is my wife.
I turned back from the light.
When she said she needed me
That's when I chose life.

And my daughter's swift invention
Came neatly to the pass.
I'd rather Claire jabbed a needle.
Than that snakes fang in my arse.

Snake Bite

A very gruesome story
I'm about to tell.
So, huddle close together.
Listen to it well.

Once I was out hunting
And made a big mistake.
Fixated on the buffalo.
I didn't see the snake.

Me and good old Roger Mac,
We're hiding by a tree.
The bastard sunk its fangs in.
Just above my knee.

(That's the snake not Roger ye ken)

The snake was verra venomous.
I began to fail,
I thought that I might die right there.
Lying on the trail.

Roger kept me going,
Good old Roger Mac,
Tied me to a homemade sledge,
And then he dragged me back.

He prayed for me in English,
The Presbyterian twit,
I like my prayers in Latin,
And there's an end to it.

Granny Claire was sore afraid,
Thinking I would pass,
The Browns had broken her syringe.
She could'na jab my arse.

She packed the wound with maggots.
Wriggly little critters,
They eat the dead infected flesh,
They quite gave me the jitters.

Grand da was in a right bad way,
I couldn't take much more,
But I had to take some action,
When yer granny fetched her saw.

She would take my leg off.
To cut off the infection,
I'd rather die with both my legs.
Was my sad reflection.

I staggered to our bedroom,
I put myself tae bed,
I waited for yer granny Claire.
To come and soothe my heid.

Yer Ma came to my rescue,
My Bree made a syringe,
She used the fangs from that old snake.
To put Claires medicine in.

It was rather painful,
She jabbed me in the wound.
Rather that than in my arse,
I yelped like a hound.

Yer Grannies penicillin,
Killed off the infection,
Ye know she is my heart and soul.
And also, my protection.

She's mended me a lot more times,
Than the sky has stars,
If ye like, and yer verra good,
I'll show ye all the scars!

Maggots and Leeches

My surgery is completed.
Though it doesn't have a door,
Most nights it's full of children.
Sleeping on the floor,

A heaving pile of kids and dogs,
Snuggled up and warm.
They'd rather sleep in one big heap,
Than observe the proper form.

An inventory of my remedies,
From mother nature's shelves
I have no modern medicines,
Most folk treat themselves.

A lively jar of maggots,
You cannot keep them long,
They very soon turn into flies,
Then they're up and gone.

The boys will fill my jar again
They search for rotting meat.
Forgotten rabbits stuck in snares,
Allow the flies a seat.

Maggots then in plenty,
They're handy for infection,
They'll clean a wound quite nicely,
If I've nothing for injection.

Ah leeches, I must keep them fed,
But only just enough,
A well-fed leach is useless,
When it comes to sucking blood,

I fish for leaches in the stream,
They live amongst the weed,
Paddle with your ankles bare,
You will catch a few indeed,

Ugly little suckers,
Their appetites I use,
A hungry leach will soon improve.
A black eye or a bruise.

Penicillin cultured.
On bread kept under glass,
In broth it's quite effective,
Or by needle – in the arse.

It's a different form of medicine.
Healing on the ridge,
Working close with nature,
And without a fridge.

My successes and my failures
Recorded in my book,
For those who may come after me
If they choose to look.

They'll see a lot of stitchings.
And birthing the odd cow.
It's a long, long way from Boston.
Two hundred years from now.

Death's door

I bid them take me up to bed,
I'd lain downstairs too long,
Fever raged around my veins.
I did nae feel too strong.

I stank like death, was hot and cold,
My head it swam and ached,
I could nae fight much longer,
Despite the jokes I made.

I feel my skin is tighter,
I feel my heart beat slow,
I feel the pull of Gods own voice,
Am I ready to let go?

Come Sassenach, please hold me,
Wrap your arms around,
Warm me, make me feel alive,
Your touch will keep me sound.

I saw a tunnel filled with light,
Like an open door,
Voices calling me to come,
Only if, I'm sure.

I felt your hands upon me,
Warm and full of life,
The choice was there, I made it.
Death or you – my wife.

'You Bastard, did you die on me!
I felt your heartbeat fade,
You were so cold, I thought you lost.
Was your decision made?

I could have gone so easily,
Twas harder still to stay,
But I know ye need me Sassenach,
Like I need you each day.

Choosing Life

Comes a time, ye ken it, aye.
When ye feel the light
When we have the choice tae die
Ye have nae will tae fight

Cut the ties and lay yer head.
Sleep forevermore.
Never tired or hungered.
Just step through the door

I felt the cold come creeping slow.
It chilled and numbed the pain.
I could ha' gone and gladly,
Then I heard ye cry ma name,

I felt ye try tae warm me,
I heard ye heart wrung calls.
Ye sore caught my attention.
When ye hand went to ma balls

Sassenach I could ha gone,
I'd severed every link.
Eternal rest awaited.
The door opened a chink.

Lie near me now and warm me.
He shall nae take me yet,
As long as I have work to do,
Ye din'nae need tae fret,

A war on the horizon,
I'm born tae lead the men.
And Sassenach ye need me.
Can ye stop yer chiding then!

And can someone kindly tell me,
What was he thinking pray,
Why on earth did Roger Mac
Let the Christie's stay,

I ken he was at Ardsmuir,
As a teacher he's of use,
Trouble surely comes in threes.
His trade is no excuse.

I'll tell ye all ye need tae know.
When I have the strength
Fetch porridge aye and honey,
For this tale is of some length

My Buffalo Gals

Shut the door, keep in out the draught,
Ach yer granny's in the kitchen,
I'm reminded of another tale,
Ye ken my leg is itching.

I was lying in my bed,
Recoverin from the snake,
I was sweatin' with a fever,
All my bones did ache,

I could see the laundry drying,
Hanging on the line,
Blowing in the autumn breeze,
The weather was quite fine,

Lizzie getting on with chores,
Jemmy by her side,
Ah my first wee grandson,
He fills me up wi pride!

I did'na see what happened next,
But I heard them scream,
Brianna running 'cross the grass.
Was this some form of dream,

A massive, woolly buffalo,
With horns, and eyes of red,
Was eyeing up Young Jemmy,
If it charged, he would be dead.

It pawed the ground and snorted,
It eyed the flapping sheet.
It heard poor Lizzie screaming,
Her terror was complete.

Ah Bree, my Bonnie, fearless lass.
The instincts of a mother,
Twas, brave the thing ye did that day,
Ye truly are my daughter,

Waving at that massive beast,
Ye face with anger filled.
I saw it throw ye in the air,
I feared ye might be killed,

I dragged myself to action,
I fell out through the door,
Naked save a blanket,
I needn't have, I'm sure.

I heard yer granny shouting,
I heard the rifles CRACK.
I saw the great beast falling,
And Bree bouncing off it's back.

I can trust my women folk,
They both can fire a rifle,
Both are pretty accurate,
With them ye do not trifle.

And I endured the wrath of Claire,
For straying from my bed,
She called me all the stupid things,
She thought of in her head.

A job now for the butcher,
There's half a ton of meat,
We wouldn't starve this winter,
We've plenty now tae eat.

I'm sure granny left some maggots,
If I may say so bold
My leg it itches like a fiend,
When the weathers cold.

That's how they killed the buffalo.
And I'm saying this in fun.
Don't mess with yer granny.
She's a danger with a gun!

Flashback to Ardsmuir

Jenny knew me taken,
That had been the plan,
I could na stand tae live my life,
Devoid of any man.

They would take the English coin,
The price upon my head,
I would go to prison.
Or I'd end up dead.

Fettered tight and in a cart,
No escape for me,
They can'nae lose Red Jamie,
They brought me here by sea.

The lurching hold, below the deck,
The rolling of the swell
I puked until I thought I'd die.
I looked as green as hell.

I crawled in chains under a bench,
Away from all around,
I wished a hole would open up,
And take me neath the ground.

The cell floor moved, alive with rats,
The stone was damp and cold,
Shivers rattled all my bones,
Here I would grow old.

A place so bleak to break a man,
Without having to endure,
Christie's pious preaching,
Welcome to Ardsmuir

The Christies arrive at Frasers Ridge

1772

The Family Christie.

The story of the Christie's
Would set your nerves a twitch.
Him a deep religious man.
And married to a witch.

Tom Christie left his family,
He sided gainst the King.
They hanged his wife for witchcraft.
Her children watched her swing.

His brother's wife was wicked.
All in the good Lords name
So, a brother brought a sister up.
He also brought her shame,

Two children living deep in need,
With no true moral guide
Feral and abandoned.
With nothing left save pride.

Tom Christie knew the truth of it,
And he would take the blame,
To save his son the gibbet,
And save his daughter's name.

Twas the son that wove the web of lies,
I would find out at the end.
There was some good in Malva,
And she thought of me as friend.

To prostitute your sister,
To cover up your sin.
Tom said the Lord find them out.
And truth at last would win.

A Broken Family

Once confined in Ardsmuir,
Indentured with the rest,
The stores man for the Jacobites,
He thought himself the best,

Set himself as leader,
The only man of letters,
Severe in his religion,
A man not kept in fetters.

A man without a presence,
A man without command,
He had never raised a sword,
To fight at Charlie's hand.

They'd found Red Jamie Fraser,
They brought him in by night,
Seasick from the journey,
And chained, lest he would fight.

Revered by all, a hero.
A leader to his core
An Officer, a papist
A warrior for sure.

And so, began a certain rift.
Of petty jealousy,
Tom Christie's nose put out of joint.
For all the men to see.

Mac Duh – son of the Black one
They'd follow him 'til death,
Inspiring of loyalty,
With every captive breath.

Seeking refuge on the ridge,
Christie swallowed pride,
Made a home amongst them.
His family at his side.

That family, who were they,
he does'nae have a wife,
His children left abandoned,
Neglected, scarred for life.

A son who raised his sister,
Without a moral stitch
They who watched their mother swing,
Convicted as a Witch

They knew no love as children,
Their life was harsh and poor,
A father locked in prison.
To be exiled that is sure.

Is it learned or in your blood,
The power of the dark,
In the Christie children
The Devil left his mark.

Major MacDonalds Wig

Us cats are fussy in our friends,
Independent in our ways,
We come and go just as we like.
It's how we spend our days.

We love to play, we love to hunt,
We can combine the two,
if we can have a bit of fun
That is just what we'll do.

The Major has a curious thing,
It lives upon his head,
It moves sometimes like it's alive,
I'd best make sure it's dead.

I'll stalk it, and I'll pounce on it.
It's really not that big,
Then I'll claw the life from it,
That thing he calls his wig.

I'll wait until he's gone to bed.
And the wig is fast asleep,
Then I'll kill it like a mouse,
Before it makes a squeak.

Get out of here you F'ng cat,
The wig is out of sight.
He picks an item off the floor.
And throws with all his might.

As I dodge the flying boot,
That drives me from his room,
I hear my mistress laughing,
And a door creaks in the gloom.

Safe in the master bedroom,
I do what nature calls,
forget about MacDonalds wig,
I'd rather lick my balls.

Dr Rawlins Casebook

Dr Rawlins casebook
Drew me back a page,
His journey out to River Run,
A man must earn a wage.

A journey fraught with danger,
Through rain and hail and mud
The patient Aunt Jocasta.
She of Jamie's blood.

Detailed diagnosis,
Noted here to see,
But what is all this Latin,
It reads like Greek to me.

He's also treating Hector,
cystitis I am sure,
Pain on micturition,
Cranberry juice the cure!

Laudanum for sleeping,
That's parr for the course.
Hector can't be sleepwalking.
That dose should stop a horse!

We ponder on each meaning.
Intrigue and medicine fused,
A reference French, and also Gold,
Masonic symbols used.

Who is roaming River Run,
In the dark of night,
What happened to the Doctor,
Did he die of fright.

He surely was a mason,
And saw things that he feared,
He wrote them in his casebook,
And then, he disappeared.

Understanding Women

In all the times I've lain with him,
He's never touched me so,
As if he's bored, no feeling there,
Monotonous and slow.

Harsh, and with no feeling,
Going through the motions,
The penny drops, I know his mind,
Is far across an ocean.

My angry scream brings him awake,
Consciousness has dawned,
Confusion, drives him from our bed,
Frustration, I am warned!

Why ......? He does not love her,
Is he jealous of another?
Why......? He does not want her,
he knows she has a lover.

He doubts his male ability,
He tried every wile invented,
Was it him or was it her?
His pride is sorely dented.

Logic does not play a part,
His mind is slowly sinking.
Another man fulfils her,
His inner Caveman, thinking!

The fact he can't abide her,
Really doesn't matter,
His prowess between the sheets,
Male ego, he must flatter,

If he could read the female mind,
Then he would plainly see,
The problem was in Laoghaire's mind,
She knew he was with me!

Do I ever think of Frank?
The question hangs above.
Frank is dead, he is a ghost,
I do not choose to love!

Maybe we should leave our ghosts,
They may just find each other,
Laoghaire with the ghost of Frank
Now there's a thought my lover.

Stop beating on your caveman chest,
Stop taking all the blame,
Women are a fickle breed,
We are not all the same.

And if you love THIS woman,
There's no more to be said!
It's bloody cold, I'm freezing!
Take me back to bed!

The Search for Steven Bonnet 1772

Myrtle Berries

Two buckets and a picnic,
Equipment for the day,
Loaded in a goat cart,
The goat refused to play,

Foraging for berries
Just to pass the time,
Don't worry for our menfolk,
That would be a crime.

An ancient flintlock pistol,
We must beware of snakes,
What else hides in the bushes
Let's go for goodness sakes,

Soft footsteps in the Myrtle,
A voice smooth as a sonnet,
Smuggler, pirate, robber,
Rapist, Stephen Bonnet.

Someone shoot him, do it now!
A knife held to my throat,
If I must die, he shall not take.
My kin back to his boat.

Children run, Jemmy hide,
The pistol leaves his waist.
The flintlock fires, chaos reigns
All sense of calm erased.

Not your son! Her voice is clear,
Her steps soft on the sand,
Stephen is your powder dry,
His pistol in her hand.

Brianna takes a careful aim,
his Irish bluff she calls,
His weapon primed, her aim is good,
Bonnets has no balls.

October 1772 Young Ian Returns

Tulach Ard

Working in the woodland,
A new pen for the hogs
Jemmy had escaped his mum,
To help us carry logs,

A hoard of stolen biscuits,
Smeared upon his face,
Smelling sweet with honey
He toddled round the place,

Big Pig! he cried, and there it was.
A boar of massive size,
With tusks as long as Jemmy's arm,
Bloodshot piggy eyes.

It looked at us and grunted.
Then Jemmy screamed in fright,
In a flash the boar had charged,
Into my line of sight,

Roger Mac had dived on it,
To wrestle it away
Then I screamed out Tulach Ard,
Grand da to save the day.

I drew my dirk, I crouched to fight,
I saw it shake its head,
One slip one fall, one careless move,
Grand da would be dead.

Here ye great fat f'er,
I challenged it to fight,
It ran at me with tusks outstretched,
I lunged with all my might.

Then I slipped and dropped the dirk,
I felt a few ribs crack,
A fence post speared it in the side,
The boar still fought us back.

Jemmy stop, ye can'nae help,
He toddled t'wards the beast,
The boar stopped still and licked its chops,
Waiting for a feast.

Then came a wolf to join the fray,
Growling fit to burst,
Attacks the boar with gnashing teeth,
I'm glad it got there first.

A whistling thump, then silence,
The arrow hit its mark,
An Indian standing silent,
Emerging from the dark.

Wolves and then a Mohawk
And a very big dead hog.
A closer look, brings sure relief,
It's Ian and his dog.

Welcome home! My nephew,
A timely entrance that,
We've bacon for at least a month,
Let's away and chew the fat.

Grand Da has Balls.
(Genetics Simplified)

So, we sat and talked genetics,
Who could travel, who could not,
Who could neatly roll their tongue,
Depends what gene you got.

The Opal had exploded,
Hot in Jems small hand,
But cold to Ian and Jamie,
Not glowing like a brand.

Ovaries and Testes,
The roll of eggs and sperm,
The boys are looking sheepish,
In fact, they start to squirm.

Talking of such matters,
Is making Jamie blush,
I never thought him prudish,
But he's having quite a flush.

Out of the mouths of children,
What's testes came the cry,
'Yer balls' replied his father,
And Grand Da thought he'd die.

Maybe Grand Da 'll show ye,
He's the one wearing a kilt,
Ian got four pen'orth in,
Blood was nearly spilt.

And so, the boys all left the room.
In the middle Jems small figure
Tell me Grand Da – you got balls?
'Aye – but yer Da's are bigger'!

Stones of Ardsmuir

Broken, beaten, worn with work.
Preached at every day,
Enough tae drive a sane man mad,
Not follow Gods good way.

Inflated like a big wee toad,
Spouting for his Lord,
The more he shouts the less they heed.
Any of his words.

A man may work his self tae death,
With peat and heavy rocks,
But constant penance on his ears,
Is one too many shocks.

What point to fight between ourselves,
We need a common ground,
This wee proud man will spread dissent.
No peace will e'er be found.

And Quarry is a yes man,
He'd like a quiet life,
Get this posting over with,
Avoid all form of strife!

A handshake with a subtlety,
A level and a square,
The Pope is not in Ardsmuir,
As if he'd think I care.

A prison lodge of masons,
Forbids the men to fight,
No politics, no talk of gods,
And we'll have peace tonight.

Deflated, with his nose put out,
His pride would fester long,
Those cold stone walls won't chill his ire,
His preaching will go on.

To all the men of Ardsmuir
Come settle on the Ridge.
A home so far from Scotland,
Your common bond a bridge

Here he came, with Fisher folk.
To settle on my land
Still preaching loud to burn yer ears,
A Bible in his hand.

Listen hard and listen well,
There's welcome here for sure,
Tom Christie ye will keep the peace,
For here my word is law.

Written for Caleb Reynolds who plays Aiden McCallum in Season Six

Fisher Folk

My Da was of the fisher folk.
We din'nae farm the land,
Fishermen not hunters
No rifle in our hand.

We travelled to the Colonies,
To start our lives anew,
On the way my Da died,
What are we to do.

Now there's only me and Ma
And my little brother
I'm scared I want my old home,
I do not want another.

This new place is in the trees,
So far from the sea,
How will we fare, what will we do?
My brother, Ma, and me

Tom Christy is a scary man.
He'd have us build for God,
We have no roof above our heads,
He does nae think that odd.

Mr Frasers word is law.
He welcomes us to stay,
But we must build cabins.
Before a place to pray

They give us food; they find us clothes.
For those that have the least
Invite us to their big fine house.
There is to be a feast.

I want to run away and hide,
I sit upon the stairs,
A big man with a big black beard,
The friendliest of stares

Tells me I'm a man now.
I must look out for Ma.
And he'll help us build a cabin.
Cos, I din nae have a Da.

He bid me eat and drink my fill.
Make ourselves at home.
To see my Ma her face lit up.
A cabin of her own.

And there are lots of children.
Lots of us to play.
Maybe I could like this place,
Yes – me and Ma will stay!

Indian Agent 1773

Coming Home

They took me in, they made me theirs,
To them I gave my soul
There I loved a woman,
She that made me whole.

Their God, he who sees everything.
Saw it was not right,
My spirit did not meet with hers,
Mine would not win the fight.

My child, one I called Iseabail,
Was buried with no name,
I never even saw her,
Dead before she came.

They cast me out, sent me back,
Go live with my kin,
Family is where ye come,
For they must let you in.

Uncle, where do souls go.
Is she condemned to roam,
Must she wander endlessly?
Nameless with no home,

We knelt beside the river,
We talked of what God planned.
That Faith was there beside her,
Would find her, take her hand.

Her spirit was not nameless.
Her name was in his heart.
He would hold her sacred,
Her journey home would start.

A name is not what matters,
I have used more than a few,
Who you are is in your heart,
Your deeds are what marks you.

To do what's right when all is lost.
When all you feel is pain,
Forgive, allow the sores to heal,
'T Will go against the grain.

Find the way to ease your mind,
Accept God has a plan,
Lord knows we may not see it yet,
You will be the bigger man.

A restless night

Heads I win, tails you lose,
I always get the bed,
Ian's coin is loaded,
He sleeps on the floor instead.

Snowbird is a canny chief,
He asks the King for guns,
But his men will kill without them,
When more raiders come.

I was thinking of the feel of home,
And drifting off to sleep,
A strong light hand upon my balls,
Caused my mind to leap,

Hell, there's a woman in my bed,
Ifrinn there may be two,
Nephew – tell them they should go!
I've no words for what to do.

I'm flattered that they honour me,
But I am not the King,
I would nae say I'm well endowed,
Hmmm tis nae small thing!

It's raining hard, they can'nae leave,
Uncle, they must stay,
And they are staying in yer bed,
I think ye'd better pray.

That night I hardly slept a wink,
I'd one hand on my kit
A man's cock has no conscience.
Mine was fighting back a bit!

Lying flat upon my back,
I prayed for some restraint,
An Indian lass on either side,
And a cock stiff in complaint!

Making Hay

Long grass cut and left to dry,
Shaken in the sun,
Turned until tis golden.
Hard work but there's fun,

Done with scythe and pitchfork,
Toil to break your back,
No machine of modern day,
To cart it down the track.

Every tenant plays their part.
In gathering the crop,
Only when the barns are full,
Is it time to stop.

Our livestock will eat well this year,
The winter feed is stored,
This is a fact of farming life.
That cannot be ignored.

time to eat, and time to drink.
Cool cider from the well,
Meat cooked overnight in pits,
The women weave their spell.

Laughing, joking, singing,
Here and there a fight,
This scene of rural carnage,
May go on 'til it's light.

One by one exhausted men,
With not the strength to roam
Lie Sleeping curled up on the grass,
Til their women take them home.

And here's Major MacDonald,
I don't mean to get rude,
His call timed to perfection.
If he came for food.

He won't get much sense from Himself,
With food and drink replete,
The exhausted red-haired Scotsman
Is sleeping at my feet.

He smells of hay and horse and sweat,
Of cider and of meat,
A small smile of contentment,
Makes the look complete.

The Majors messages can wait,
He curls up in a ball,
A cheeky wink shows him awake,
But not here for this call.

The Major is persistent,
But plied with food and drink,
Surveys the farming idyll,
His formal manners shrink,

And at my feet, there's snoring,
A gentle nasal rattle,
The rigours of a long hard day,
Hay making wins the battle.

Goodbye Iseabail

I watched the rivers endless flow,
The anger left my bones.
Running onward to the sea,
Clear water over stones

I sat, I prayed, I talked with them,
The spirits of my life,
The Murray's and the Mohawk,
My daughter and my wife.

Some not dead but in my mind,
Constant in my brain,
Those that sought to comfort,
Those that caused me pain,

There I found forgiveness.
There I found my soul.
There I found an inner strength,
That thing that keeps us whole.

Emily no longer mine.
Be happy in your life.
I wish you many children,
May all be free of strife.

And you my Mohawk brother,
Make sure you love her well.
There is a small place left in me,
That would see you in hell.

Carved with love, I blessed the wolf,
I laid it in the race,
Baptised it for you Iseabail,
I never saw your face.

I leave you here with all our Gods,
Whichever one you choose,
I'm sure they are all really one,
Just seen from different views,

You are not lost and wandering,
Like some discarded wraith,
A guiding hand will find your soul,
My uncle sends you Faith.

The Call of Faith

Iseabail, I see you,
A path for you is planned.
In the world ethereal
Come and take my hand.

We walk beside our kinfolk.
We watch them from above,
Hold the prayers they send us.
Answer them with love,

Fly with me in spirit,
We never shall grow old,
One day the quick will join us,
In Gods eternal fold.

Family awaits you,
Tiny Mohawk wraith
You will never be alone.
Cousin, I am Faith.

Time on earth is transient,
Must always have an end,
Spirit has no boundaries.
On Faith you may depend.

Anaesthetics

The ability to operate.
Without the patient screaming,
A body lying limp, relaxed.
In a state of dreaming.

Copious quantities of drink
Will help to stay the nerves,
But it will not stop the pain,
It taxes the reserves.

Laudanum will induce a sleep,
But also brings a frown,
The patient needs restraining still,
Sometimes tying down.

The brave will suffer surgery.
With a gag between their teeth,
Screaming through their rigid jaws
To find some slight relief.

The art of making ether,
Using its sweet vapour,
Will send the strongest man to sleep.
But do not light a taper!

More complicated surgery
Can then be undertaken.
With the patient sleeping peaceful
But please don't be mistaken.

Ether is a fickle thing.
Its synthesis is danger,
Alcohol and Vitriol
Are better kept as strangers,

High risk of explosion,
Greater risk of fire,
One degree on either side
Can land you in the mire.

So, I make it in the shed,
And hope that no stray spark
Blows me into smithereens,
While working in the dark.

There is one good chemist.
Who makes It, unafraid?
A soldier's cure for seasickness
He sells It ready made.

The Devils Genes

Lucifer – light bearer
Mistress, what's it for?
Phosphorus glows in oxygen,
The devils light for sure,

A mind confused by preaching,
Mixed with superstition,
Earnest eyes seek answers,
What really is her mission.

Instructed how to fear her god,
Not taught more than she needs
Religion, history, and prayer
Just who planted this seed.

He does not teach her science,
Her curious mind might light,
What's in her bone and in her blood.
Just may win that fight.

She has no fear of seeing death,
She seeks control of life,
I could teach her healing,
But her father would cause strife.

He is a man of learning,
Why does he hold her back?
What does he fear is in this child,
That makes her outlook black.

Her dabbling in science,
Helping with my healing,
Her interest in macabre things,
He sees the devils dealing.

Time will tell the story,
Tom will spill the beans,
His wife, her mother was a witch.
She has the devils' genes!

Matches

Lit up with excitement,
A tiger poised to pounce.
Brianna's eyes are fiery proud,
She's something to announce.

Jumping to conclusions,
Suspense will drive them wild,
Please calm down, the lot of you!
I am not 'with child.'

Lucifer light bearer
Phosphorus in the dark
Exposed to air it will ignite.
Without even a spark

Fire at your fingertips
Flames upon a stick,
Easier than striking flint.
When you light a wick.

Tumbleweed went round the room.
Why would that excite!
We are adept at lighting fires,
This won't our minds ignite.

Doubt is always forefront.
They don't like what is new,
Suspicious minds are thinking.
This is the devil's brew.

They'd celebrate a baby,
Now here comes the catch,
They really have no interest.
In the lighting of a match.

Da can see its uses,
Roger is quite proud,
Claire will use them always,
They voice support aloud.

A fiery re-creation,
Its history will cast.
A trail of destruction
From the future to the past,

Understanding Men

Both had been imprisoned,
Both honourable men,
Neither one will give an inch.
Like rams fenced in a pen,

Butting heads, a contest,
Which one is the stronger,
I'd bet Mr Fraser,
Will last out the longer,

I'd sewn up Tom Christie's hand,
With no pain relief,
With Jamie there he would not flinch
He'd groan through gritted teeth,

They play a game of cat and mouse,
Verbal barbs, and taunts,
One mentions honour in his scars,
One Bible knowledge flaunts.

Each testing the other,
They fight with verbal swords,
Who will lose their cool to temper,
In this game of words,

Christie has the last word.
Going through the door,
But Jamie's laughing – eyebrow raised,
He's seen it all before.

Opposite in many ways,
But really just the same,
Men like Christie needed,
If we are to win the game.

I don't think I can understand,
Why they never stop.
The constant competition,
The need to be on top.

Sassenach don't fool yourself,
You ken us all too well,
You'd like to think you din'nae,
For it is the road to hell.

Tom Christie is a fighter,
When his nose is out of joint,
He'll fight hard to keep his place,
And that is just the point.

Malva

Curious, intelligent,
A willingness to learn,
But does she have a caring side,
That is a concern?

Brought up by her father,
A strict, religious man,
Kicking at the traces,
Does she have a plan?

Claire has taken her to heart,
Is this a mistake,
Will our heroine survive?
The trouble this girl makes.

Abused by her brother,
Was she willing? Did he make her?
Malva Christie – troubled soul?
Or merely trouble maker!

The Devils Pact

Enquiring mind,
Intelligent
Quick to learn her work.
Enthralled
Enthusiastic
True colours soon unfurled,
Curious,
And watchful
Sharp of hand and eye,
Nothing good
Will come of you.
If through the latch you spy.
Watching
stolen moments
Noting every act
Plotting
Scheming
In your mind

The devil makes his pact.

Pain Relief

A stubborn man, set in his mind.
Tis the healing craft of witches,
To feel no pain, the sleep of death,
To wake up then, with stitches.

He did not trust, he had no faith,
Though faith had set his mind,
He'd not submit to witchcraft,
In that way he was blind.

He sat there stoic in the chair,
Reciting Bible verse,
While Jamie's strength held muscle still
I heard Tom Christie curse.

Leather strop between his teeth,
He bit for all his worth.
Through gritted teeth he called his Lord,
Questioning his birth

The operation simple,
But off the scale of pain
To free the tendons of his hand,
So, he could write again.

And so, I operated,
Between two stubborn men
Neither one was giving in,
A respect was born right then.

Biblical his knowledge
Of Presbyterian curse
Tom Christie used the whole damn book.
As the pain got worse

He could have taken ether,
But that would take some trust,
He'd rather sit and curse the Lord,
And suffer as he must.

The Right Hand of the Lord

He'd sat and waited patient.
Amongst the drama of that day,
His reasons kept close to his chest,
Would make young Malva pay.

No longer could he wield the strap,
He would not spoil the child!
Spare the girl the punishment,
For her mother being beguiled.

He would have the surgery,
And he would take the pain,
Repair his hand so he may have.
The use of it again.

Jamie pinned him to the chair.
And read aloud from the Psalms.
The right hand doeth valiantly
Tom Christie has no qualms.

The papist and the Protestant
Both quote the word of God,
Screamed aloud through gritted teeth,
Would often sound quite odd.

Soft words for the sutures,
We're round the final bend,
Walking in Deaths Valley,
The lords house at the end.

Silken stitches finished,
The end of my endeavour,
Just as they reached those pearly gates,
To dwell within forever.

Goodness, oh and mercy,
May help him through these pains,
They are but words, they do not live.
In Thomas Christie's veins.

The Ballad of James McCready

Groping hands on filthy floor,
Searching in the dark,
Eyes grown weak through lack of light,
Young – yet to make his mark.

A lock of hair, a precious thing
A tie with loved ones lost,
A locket one last token thing
Reminds him of the cost.

A stuttering apology,
Sir, I'm going blind,
Memory of his young wife's face,
He cannot bring to mind.

Christie bids me think of God,
Soldier for his cause,
Have we lost all for nothing then,
Must we accept these laws.

I hear men say your wife is 'gone'
But you remember well,
How do you keep her memory
Mine is a broken spell,

Close your eyes, you'll see her,
Her image will come in.
We have loved like others can't,
That cannot be a sin.

Comfort given in the dark,
To men with whom he bled,
And in the bitter feuding,
James McCready dead,

Here's a bit o' tartan.
To take ye to yer grave,
Someone must be punished.
For Auld Charlie's act sae brave.

Tis mine – the voice commanded,
Once more he shed his sark,
Christie saw the silvered scars,
Which marked his back like bark.

Silently he took the lash,
Instead of that poor fool,
And quietly the Ardsmuir men
Came back under his rule.

Tom Christie cannot see it,
He'd have auld Charlie flogged,
This is not justice Fraser.
The answer – Is it not!

The Pope is nae in Ardsmuir.
In Prison with my men
There is a supreme being.
In my beliefs ye ken.

Become a lodge of Masons.
Quarry saw the point,
Leaving Thomas Christie
A nose well out of joint

Loneliness of men

How can a soul be lonely,
In a cell with fifty men,
Human presence always there,
But no company ye ken,

By day there is unending toil,
The hunger and the cold,
By night, the fruitless search for sleep,
The snores and grunts and groans,

Sometimes a little comfort,
A letter shared from home,
A tale told in the darkness,
The moonlight through the gloom.

Fights break out o'er nothing,
Man reaches out for man,
Seeking out some comfort,
They will find it where they can,

Those nights I lay there so alone,
If sleep would only come,
Then I could call you to my dreams,
Again, we could be one.

No other man would touch me,
Ye, see You recollect.
I was McDubh, I was their Chief,
They had too much respect.

Sometimes lying like a dog,
Twitching in my dreams,
Craving for a hand to touch,
Heart bursting at the seams,

Sassenach you feel my dreams,
You understand them plain.
I sleep well with you by my side,
Not lonely or in pain.

Let me hold you through my darkness,
Where my demons still survive,
Your touch can drive them from my mind,
And make me feel alive.

The vision of the sacred heart,
In Paris came to mind,
The loneliness of Jesus,
Reaching out to all mankind

Rape

No good comes from Brownsville.
And all of it's called Brown,
They all know how to bear a grudge.
And Lionel wears the Crown.

A violent and a cruel man
He loves a good vendetta.
He doesn't like the Frasers,
I think he should know better.

Taken from the surgery.
A bag upon my head,
Trussed up like a turkey.
Sure, I'd soon be dead,

The still was a diversion.
To draw the men away.
Lionel Brown had sworn he would.
Be back another day.

The vile names they called me,
They are skilled at abuse,
To violate a woman
They don't need an excuse.

The Brown gang took their turns at me.
Then tied me hand and foot.
They left me there so I would die.
An ant under his foot,

I lost myself in music,
Escaped into my head,
Tried to find a happy place.
While all my reason fled.

My rescue wasn't pretty,
Military precision.
No reprieve, kill them all.
I heard the last decision.

One survived the rescue,
That was Lionel Brown.
They took him to the Surgery.
And there they tied him down.

I was lost inside my shell,
My outside wounds would heal,
The bruises very soon would fade.
The open wounds would seal.

Once, Jamie said his Inner man.
Laid bare, had hurt his soul.
And had to build a shelter.
Before it could be whole.

With Lionel in my surgery
With Marsali by his bed,
Mentally I found some wood.
And started on my shed.

Brave Wee Thing

I'd thought tae be so gentle,
Bring her back to peace,
Soothe her body and her mind,
But her demons I release,

Wine tae blur the memories,
Wine tae dim the light,
Wine will draw her from her shell.
wine will make her fight,

Blood-stained lips and raking teeth,
Clawing, raking nails,
Urge me to a darker place.
A place where reason fails,

Sweat soaked muscles strained in need,
Scent of untamed lust,
Locked together, fused as one.
We grind ourselves to dust,

Brave wee thing, I feel you rise,
Your spirit fights with mine,
You are here, you are whole.
Now live, not just survive.

My silent tears will mix with yours
As your demons watch you weep,
This sobbing wretch will cry with you,
Even as we sleep.

Faithfulness

Yer fierce as a badger,
More grizzly than a bear,
Prouder yes than lucifer,
And now ye have no hair,

Patience – ken ye have none.
Kindness – din'nae jest,
Yer terrifying ruthless
When yer at yer best.

Female attributions
I fear that ye have none,
Well, none that I can count on,
Now yer arse is skin and bone.

I can'nae list yer virtues.
All I need tae know,
Is you being there beside me,
And that ye'll never go.

Yer verra kind and verra clean,
But not much of a cook,
I've seen ye burn the supper.
Yer nose stuck in a book.

Should ye die and leave me,
I should be very sore,
I'd argue with the devil,
Tae let ye live some more.

Hair will grow, flesh will return.
Your beauty will not fade,
You still outshine the sun itself.
Ye put it in the shade.

Eyes like well-aged whisky
With a dash of honey
Ye tend to my wee scratches.
Sometimes ye think me funny!

What is it draws me to ye,
We'll all of the above,
Yer faithfulness above them all,
And loyalty, and love.

Over Your Shoulder

I see you Mrs Fraser
Trying to do good,
Knives so sharp and words to match.
You do more than you should.

I watch you mistress healer.
I haunt your every day.
I live inside your conscience.
I will not go away.

Hedgewhore, you had it coming.
You got what you deserved.
Corrupting our good women,
We had our justice served.

Hear me Dr Rawlings
The consequences fear,
Our wives are property to use,
You should not interfere.

You see me in your surgery,
You feel me in your house,
As you creep for your 'cup of tea'
Quiet as a mouse.

I am the voice inside your head,
That calls you to that mask.
The sleep that makes you rid of me,
The Oblivion you ask.

A shadow in your surgery,
Your sanctuary breached,
Nowhere now for you to hide.
Where your soul cannot be reached.

So run to that great man of yours
The one that is your world,
I follow you close on your heels.
While in his arms you're curled

There will be a vengeance,
It will ride into town,
My brother, he will keep his word,
Beware of Richard Brown

Little Boxes.

Folded up and packed away,
The troubles of the past
Every small mistake I made.
From first one to the last.

Sealed inside an inner wall.
The box lid nailed down tight.
Stored away in corners dark.
Far away from light.

With hollow voice he reaches
Breaking through the dark
Lionel Brown is whispering.
His taunting leaves it's mark.

No longer hiding from me.
His calling becomes bolder.
All the past he waves at me,
His ghost is at my shoulder.

Every life I ever touched,
Every life I changed.
He turns the good to evil,
All is rearranged.

All I did for love of you.
Is trampled into dust,
No longer can I face myself.
In the mirror of the just.

Never ending voices call
And I do what they ask.
Just one drop and then one more
Take refuge in the mask.

I see your eyes awash with tears.
As I push you away,
I'm fighting what I have become,
My demons out to play.

Easier if I were gone.
It is as if I lied,
I thought the thoughts, but not the deed.
The day that Malva died.

A cup of tea will cure all ills.
The kettle calls the pot,
Blackness fills my very soul,
I'm English not a Scot.

Sassenach don't fight me,
There is refuge in my arms,
Not bottled in your surgery,
Break free of ethers charms,

All the good that you have done,
Is here before your eyes,
How can ye think so foolish lass,
Ye are intelligent and wise,

The ridge exists because of you,
And may God damn their soul?
It's you who heals their bodies,
Keeps their families whole.

Let me fight your ghosts my love.
As you fought mine before
I will fight the devil.
Should he turn up at my door

Hear the echo of the past,
He will do what he must,
The time has come and Richard Brown
Will turn the dreams to dust!

I've Taken no Such Oath

My mother called her English whore,
My mother called her bitch,
Had her tried at Cranesmuir.
Wanted her burned, a witch.

I remember well the big stramash,
When Claire came back for daddy,
My mother tried to shoot him.
She was in such a paddy.

I've lived with them for many years,
I see they love each other,
And now I've come to look at Claire.
As if she were my mother.

When they came and kidnapped her,
They knocked me to the floor,
I was heavy still with child,
Yet still they called me whore.

Claire has taught me many things.
Of the art of healing,
The thought of healing Lionel Brown
Was not that appealing.

I prepared for him a potion.
I told him it would heal.
If he lay still and drank it,
Then he'd have a meal.

He would not have to drink it,
I did not have to check,
With one swift move I jabbed it,
Into the big vein in his neck.

His death was almost instant.
Quicker than a gun,
Claire's oath said she'd not harm him.
But I've not taken one!

The Mask of Sleep

Sweet sleep
A few drops on the mask
Perhaps a few drops more
Erase the pictures from the past,
The pain you can't ignore.

Breathe deep.
To lie oblivious
If only for a while
Blank out the racing of your mind.
Blot out all that's vile.

Sweet dreams
Ride on waves of hope
Hide away from life.
Refuge here from darkness
Refuge here from strife

Inhale
Descend into the depths.
Picture all you love.
Shut out the hurt, shut out the pain,
Let that go on above.

One drop more
Will take you there.
One sweet drop on the mask
One drop to oblivion
If that is what you ask

He calls you.
Do not spoil the rush,
Don't let him see your cure.
secrecy imperative
If these dreams are to endure

He wakes you.
From my cloying fumes
He breaks sweet smelling dreams.
Pulls you to reality.
Did he not hear your screams?

Secrets
You make room for me,
For me to him you lie
Convince him you are in control.
I will not let you die.

Don't Listen
You are deaf to him.
I've stolen all your pain.
Locked it in my walls of glass.
And you will seek me again.

Next time
I will call you.
When nightmares ring your bell
Sweet sleep in a bottle
I am the road to hell.

Come Back Sassenach

Sassenach, I worry,
It is nae sitting well,
The sleep ye seek, unnatural,
Yet ye fall under its spell,

I ken yer mind is troubled,
Tell me what is wrong.
A trouble shared; a trouble halved.
With two we're twice as strong.

I feel ye leave my side at night.
Ye creep around the house,
Ye think ye do it quiet,
But yer too large for a mouse.

Talk to me, tell me your pain,
Let us talk it through,
Don't lock away your demons,
For then they stay with you.

When I awake, and you are gone,
ye've sneaked off to that place.
Yer chemical oblivion
With that mask o'er yer face.

The space I feel beside me,
Cold under the covers,
Do not let your shadows,
Force us apart as lovers.

Answer me please Sassenach.
I beg ye tell me why,
I fear for our future,
I fear that you may die.

Time will dim the demons,
Forgiveness numbs the pain,
I would kill them all fer you,
To have ye back again.

I will not let ye do this,
Once you saved my soul,
Shall I stop ye making ether,
If that will keep ye whole.

I can nae lie alone at night,
Where once ye laid yer head,
Reaching out for comfort,
In a cold and empty bed.

One Hand

Milord has kept the oath he made,
To him I am a son,
Married to his daughter,
Hands – I have but one!

I am not a farmer,
I cannot work the land,
There is nothing on The Ridge,
For a Frenchman with one hand.

My wife is always pregnant,
But I cannot provide,
Scornful when she looks at me,
It makes me die inside.

Tis she that tends the children,
And she that tends the beasts,
The house, the home, she cooks and cleans.
And I contribute least.

Her kinfolk thinks me lazy,
Or look at me with pity.
A Frenchman born and Paris bred.
I'm better in the city.

My refuge is the Whisky still,
A place where I can hide,
Taste the product as it's made,
Liquor now my bride.

A black cloud lives over my head,
It permeates my soul,
Nothing will bring lightness back,
Oblivion my goal.

When all around are toiling,
I'm drunk - can barely stand,
I am ashamed, I am no use,
I only have one hand.

Things I know are said in jest,
Are arrows to my heart,
Dark despair has landed,
Never to depart.

Fergus, do not work so hard,
Sampling the wares.
Marsali needs you home with her,
She's worn away with cares.

Fergus, watch the weans,
Fergus milk the goat,
This is not work for a man.
Man's work should be of note!

Milord is losing patience,
For he sees a lot,
And now he sees his son of heart,
Become a drunken sot.

Fergus Man!!

Fergus man, where are ye,
The bairn is on the way.
Ye should be there beside her,
Not hiding away,

Fergus man, get up there,
Put the bottle down,
Yer wife could be in danger,
Stop acting like a clown.

Marsali does not need me,
She'll be fine with Claire,
She will not even notice,
If I am not there,

Fergus man, she calls for you,
She needs you by her side,
Get off your arse and be the man.
Who took that girl to bride,

The birth does not go easy,
Her husband should be there,
You will nae forgive yerself.
If she thinks ye did not care,

Fergus man, sober up.
Ye whisky sodden tool,
Must I take ye there myself,
Ye wee Parisian fool.

She loves ye man, she calls for you,
Things are not tae plan,
Get yersel tegither!
Ye aggravating man.

Roger laid the law down,
Took Fergus by the scruff,
Hot foot back to Marsali,
Will he be soon enough!!

Mother Claire

We've come a long way mother Claire.
Since that awful day,
When ma shot da in jealous rage
Tae make ye go away,

I hated you for ages.
For taking da away,
Mother said you haunted them.
She could'na make him stay.

I see just how he loves ye,
That love went on and on
Surviving all the hardships
In the years that you were gone

Mother told us ye were evil.
Said ye were a witch,
Wished ye dead at every turn,
She really loved to bitch.

Fergus keeps me pregnant,
I've bairns and some tae spare,
And when the next one comes along
I ken you will be there.

I love ye like a mother,
Trust ye with my life,
And as for da, my mother knew.
Ye'd always be his wife.

Master of Mushrooms

Milady, you have no idea.
I saw the life they lead.
Seen as freaks of nature.
Thought the devils seed,

You say we can protect him,
He is part of our hive,
What happens though when we are gone,
How will he survive,

I tell you now of Paris,
Before I met Milord,
The morels and the Chanterelles
Abused for bed and board,

A sexual perversion,
An oddity for hire,
Valued only for their flesh,
Sold for man's desire.

I had a friend amongst them,
Until I found him slain
Discarded with his throat cut,
In a sewage filled back lane,

The madame took his body,
Luc has no final rest.
His organs sold in pickle jars,
To be a source of jest.

My son can have no future,
In a superstitious land
How can I protect him,
When I only have one hand.

I fear for him Milady,
What work can he do?
We are as useless as each other.
And you must see it too.

Resurrection

It never pays to go against
the wishes of the dead,
They may come back an haunt ye,
If ye dinna see folk fed.

The body wrapped inside the shroud,
She made it as a bride,
Brought it far from Scotland.
Her body it would hide.

Jaw strapped shut with linen,
Eyes drawn down and closed.
Salt and bread beside her,
Quiet in repose.

Old Hiram was a tightwad.
Purse strings pulled up tight.
He saw no need to celebrate,
To set the spirits right.

'I am the resurrection'!
She opened up her eyes,
Granny Wilson is alive,
There's screaming and surprise.

Sitting in her coffin,
Berating Hiram Crombie
With all the folk around her,
Who think they've seen a zombie.

Where is the food? where is the drink?
This is not a wake!
And where is my good, jewelled brooch.
That was nae yours to take.

Himself produced the Whisky,
Mrs Bug the food,
It pacified the angry corpse.
Lightened up her mood.

Precious few the minutes,
Before she really died,
At least she went in knowledge.
Of what had been supplied.

She did'na think she'd she the day,
She said with some finality,
When she'd be laid to final rest
With papist hospitality

Mixed Metaphors

They must have talked of music.
Of the future kind,
Heavy Metal, Rock, and Roll
He is musically blind.

Awoken in the morning.
With me upon a plate
He really couldn't get enough.
And he couldn't wait.

The joys of lubrication,
What a way to wake,
I suppose I was quite Thunderstruck.
I'm not a girl to fake!

Watching from the bedclothes,
While I tame my hair,
Greased lightening ay then Sassenach
I get the deep blue stare!

My, he loves a metaphor,
This one makes me laugh,
Greased lightening is not really praise,
It's far too quick by half!

Beware of the Pig!!

In the quest for plumbing,
Roger dug the hole,
A kiln and lots of pipe work,
Was Brianna's goal.

I stood with Roger at its edge,
Chatting, digging done
When good Major Macdonald,
Entered in the fun.

He hadn't seen her coming,
Creeping from her den
Prowling round the corner,
She puts terror into men!

Pig! Shouted Roger –
as best his voice could do,
Pig! I shouted louder,
The Major heard me too.

He broke into a gallop,
Running from the sow,
She grunted and she snuffled,
And followed him, and how.

Running at the double,
This is no time to talk,
The Major trying to escape,
Five hundred pounds of pork.

Pit! We screamed together,
The Major turned his head,
Spurs entangled in his boots,
He fell down just like lead.

The sow was gaining on him,
Back up and run away,
Heading for the kiln pit,
There's not much we could say.

We saw him as he disappeared,
Straight over the edge,
Curled up like a hedgehog,
Protecting meat and veg!

Are ye damaged Major?
His wig was still in place,
Expecting to be eaten,
Said the look upon his face!

Din'nae worry Major,
She's given up on that,
Climb out of there in safety,
She's chewing on yer hat!

Calls in the Forest – a Cry for Help

Sat around the fire,
The pipe had gone around,
Stories told of battles,
Some fought on far off ground.

Beer and food and mellow smoke,
And talk of homeland lost,
I began to talk about that time,
The killing and the cost.

Fourteen men, I counted,
I could not call one to mind,
What sort of memory is this?
That makes such killing blind.

Back upon that rain-soaked moor,
My face with tears is sodden,
The earthy smell of peat and gorse,
Weeping for Culloden.

When all but Bird had gone to bed,
I told him of my fears.
That my women saw the future
The awful trail of tears.

Now Bird has sent his mother,
To warm me in my bed,
This is no sense of humour,
She has come to clear my head.

Talk to me Bear Killer,
I will comb your hair,
I hear your words in any tongue,
Your mind I will repair,

The words came out in Gaelic,
To her I bared my soul,
The spectres Grief and Loss and Fear,
The things that kept me whole,

I felt my spirit rising,
And floating up above,
My voice came from a distance,
Softer than a dove.

They will no longer haunt you,
No evil in my heart,
Not here, not now, in this place peace,
At least that is a start.

She combed the tangles from my mind,
Healing words she spoke,
All thoughts of vengeance on that time,
Dispersing with the smoke.

Trail of Tears

What then will become of us,
When the wars are done,
When the Kings men have all gone,
And independence won,

Will they let us live in peace?
Not take away our land,
Must we arm ourselves again,
Make another stand.

The white man he wants everything.
He takes without consent.
He rapes the land of all its wealth,
His greed is never spent.

He takes our sacred mountains,
He kills without restraint,
No respect for bird or beast
Or for a man of paint.

My brothers they will send you far,
Make you leave your home,
Do not believe their promises,
They will not let you roam,

Independence at a cost,
What the sacrifice
For white men are not tolerant
Your lives will be the price.

Banished from your homelands.
Away from all you know,
To barren land, not fertile plain,
And you will have to go.

The journey will see many die,
Upon a trail of tears,
It will come, it has been seen,
I can't allay your fears.

Kiss them better.

To save us doing laundry,
He stripped off to the waist,
Muscled hard from working,
My request was so misplaced.

I'd seen Da's back few times before,
His shrug says 'din'nae fash.'
Years have passed but still they bring,
A memory of the lash.

We strained to move that boulder,
The children helped us NOT!
Dirty, muddy, happy,
We reached the swimming spot.

The mud fight was quite brutal,
They're clay from head to toe,
Every nook and cranny,
Filled with muck ye know.

How do they get so dirty,
Da says there's but one cure,
Dunk them in the swimming hole,
Their screams we must endure!

If ye do not let him try,
ye will nae know he can,
I wait to see if Jem can swim,
Drowning not the plan.

Holding tight to Grand Da,
Legs wrapped around his waist,
Jemmy rode home piggy back,
He saw what Grand Da faced.

Walking home he told them,
Why his back was scarred,
The boys would fight the world for him,
They told him – no holds barred.

Then Jemmy kissed that broken skin,
I heard my father wince,
Then he laughed and stretched a bit,
Recovered like a Prince,

Still a reminder of the past
A trigger in his mind
It's why he keeps his shirt on
How could I be so blind?

Still taken back into a time,
Of whip, and chain and fetter,
A child's voice behind his ear says.
'Jemmy make it better.'

The Venom of the North Wind.

Dabbling in witchcraft,
Meddling with charms,
Seeks to pull another's man.
Into her vengeful arms,

A grave disturbed, Some stolen bones,
Seaweed burned in fire,
Take the ash and sprinkle.
To hold your heart's desire,

An ancient love charm seldom used,
But where is it directed,
Who calls on these unholy words,
And who will be affected.

An old man's grave, but newly sealed
Remains fresh in the ground
Earth disturbed to find his bones,
To turn a head around.

The venom of the north wind,
Will blow cold across the land.
Will raise a storm and break the peace,
If all goes as she's planned.

They say that what is bred in blood,
Comes out in the bone,
Scheming child born of a witch
Cannot her sin atone.

She will tear a home apart,
Will weave a web of lies,
Frasers Ridge will fall in flames.
When Malva Christie dies.

There can be no justice.
Where there is no law,
And lives are tossed like flotsam,
On the rising tide of war.

Desecration

A poor old man and wasted.
His flesh hangs from his bones,
Now dead inside his shelter
Safe from praying crones,

Fed with sins ate from the dead,
A withered corpse his plate,
Life extinct will no one care,
Is he missing from Gods slate?

Was it sin that killed him?
Or maybe something worse,
A fever strong that has no cure.
An apprentice witches curse.

Bread and ale they fed him.
To keep Gods wrath at bay
To let the dead, lie peaceful.
Their sins he'd take away.

Sinister Miss Christie,
You've learned a lot I fear,
Your teacher gives you knowledge,
Your mother the idea!

Evil comes in many forms,
The devil drives your deeds,
What is it that you really seek,
What will fulfil your needs.

Morals of an alley cat,
Behaviour of a whore,
Spreading rumour on the ridge,
Damaging for sure.

Nought good will become of it,
When the good have been misled,
To save a life inside you
She will desecrate you dead.

The web you spread around you,
Will weave an evil tale,
Your mentor thrown into the fire.
With stale bread and ale.

Calling Roger Mac

It will turn ye off ye sandwich.
A look from Old Arch Bug
His face will make the milk turn.
Before it leaves the jug

A chip upon his shoulder
Like to weigh him down,
Everything a grumble
And like as not a frown.

Trouble lays on trouble,
I have nae time for lunch,
I'd find those twins and lay them out,
They're hidin' I've a hunch.

Ye say that in the future,
Some will not eat meat,
I ken ye don't like killin'
But what then would ye eat?

When I catch up with the Beardsley's
Ye ken I'll make them shiver.
Would a vegetarian
Excuse me eatin' liver.

I ken ye have a calling,
I see ye care for folk.
Kindness flowing in yer veins.
And ye can take a joke.

Follow where yer heart leads.
Where ye can do most good,
Not all men are hunters,
And they don't go short of food.

We din'nae have a minister,
We din'nae have a priest,
Tom Christies words will burn our ears.
Before his chidings ceased.

Go then, make it formal!
Get yerself ordained,
Then say one for the Beardsley Twins
Before they end up maimed.

Continental Congress

We'll drink an ale, we spar with words,
A lining up of views,
Alliances are tested.
Each man makes his dues.

Trust must be established.
If treason is the game,
I ken they have nae met me.
To Hartnett just a name.

To toast the King, with eyebrows raised
A look of great disdain,
His comrade can'nae hide his take.
Allegiance can'nae feign.

Bona Fides established,
My colours at their mast,
The Continental Congress,
Has signed me up at last.

A world of secret meeting,
When treason is in play,
One man, I cannot meet his eye,
What must I tell John Grey.

My eye drawn to the fire,
Have I come too far,
Will I end like Bonnet,
Bollocks in a Jar.

A White Rose for the British

All of town abuzz with life,
A welcome for a Scot
A migrant from the highlands
They will forget her not!

The men in full regalia
Tartan de rigeur.
Ladies in their finest
A Ceilidh to be sure!

Those that can't remember.
Love to reminisce.
Those that charged the British guns.
Would give those tales a miss.

How to address a legend,
Just say hello is best,
She's really just a person.
Just like all the rest

A legend of the 'forty-five
A white rose to the core,
Speaking now for loyalty
A turnabout for sure.

The Oath that we were made to swear,
An exodus unplanned.
Rebuilt lives and fortunes,
A new and restless land.

They will not fight for freedom,
They will fight to keep their lives,
The lands they farm, the wealth they've earned,
their kinfolk and their wives.

They have no taste for rebellion,
For they have lost before,
They thrive on tales of glory,
Remember the last war.

The English took my freedom,
I'll not again wear chains,
If I must fight again for right
I'll face the guns again.

For I know Fionnaghal!
She talks a rare, good fight,
The Bonnie Prince would pay in gold,
Would she assist his flight.

But I have better anecdotes,
I've ones tae raise a smile,
Like the day she stole my bridie,
And I pulled her hair foreby!

We met when da was buying sheep,
On the Isle of Skye,
She was nae fair or gracious,
When she poked me in the eye,

A braw wee lassie with the grippe,
And a very runny nose,
And both of us just barely seven,
My first love I suppose.

Well Jamie are you blushing,
A childhood crush you said,
On wee Flora Macdonald
My! Your ears are turning red!

Light relief

Pleasant waves of light relief
Inhaled with many sighs,
Breathe it in and it will ease
The pain behind your eyes,

It also lightens all your mood.
It may just calm your nerves.
Let you give your audience.
Just what it deserves,

Ladies come and join me,
Adjourn to pastures green.
Where we can talk and smoke the hemp.
And do so quite unseen.

Giggling with laughter
The pipe was passed around,
Together with the hip flask,
The gossip did abound,

Talk of lives forgotten
The hemp removes a blind
Memories of darker times,
Hiding in your mind.

I am the sweet sleep calling you.
Come then take a drop,
Reach out for my bottle,
I hear the stopper pop!

A small trip to oblivion
Will send the demons back,
A few drops on your handkerchief,
Will get you back on track.

Back before they miss you,
But miss you someone will,
Small lies you tell he will add up.
Then will he love you still?

Talking Ballocks

Wrinkled, insignificant.
Once his pride and joy
Nestled in his breeches,
Each side of his 'Le Roi'

Hairy orbs once sae attached.
His measure of a man
Protected and respected.
And scratched because he can!

There above the fire
Labelled and displayed.
Removed from reach of fishes.
When his final act had played

A potted curiosity
Or a message to us all
Where some are plotting treason,
And others potting balls.

Tis said that brave men have them,
They boast about the size.
I have nae yet heard Claire complain.
Of what's before her eyes.

Floating now in vinegar
Not hung between his legs
Stephen Bonnets bollocks
Like a pair of pickled eggs

We talk independence,
Freedom from the Crown,
Does this await my testicles?
When they cut me down!

Aldwych Farce

All hell is loose at River Run,
The Lieutenant came by stealth,
His hobbled horse found in a field,
To steal Jocasta's wealth.

We rode at speed from Wilmington,
Horses blown and sweated,
Filthy from the dusty road,
To find what We suspected.

Duncan Innes injured,
Lieutenant Wolff stone dead,
Ulysses gone missing,
A price upon his head.

For Ulysses, had cut Wolff's throat,
Straight from ear to ear.
If they catch him, he will swing,
On this the law is clear.

Where better for a body,
Than to hide it in a tomb,
But in with Hector Cameron's
There isn't any room.

Jamie opened up the crypt,
To find the space was taken,
The corpse of Daniel Rawlings,
If Jocasta's not mistaken.

We'll put him in yer coffin Aunt,
If I may be so bold.
But when he takes the lid off,
The coffin's packed with gold.

We will take Dr Rawlings,
To be buried on our ground
Lieutenant Wolff can take his place,
Sealed in safe and sound,

Seems we had arrived there.
In the nick of time,
Like something from an Aldwych Farce,
Clearing up the crime!

The yarn Jocasta spun us,
Was all a pack of lies!
You'll not part Hector from the gold,
Not even when he dies!

The Wind of War

Feckless individual,
Driven low to crime,
Desperate for an Avenue
To get back to his time.

Imprisoned now, a common thief,
He will await his fate,
Stolen emerald in his hand,
His ticket home – too late.

Sitting in the shadows
The darkness of the jail
Killing time and waiting
His mission doomed to fail.

Help me fellow traveller,
Would she help him from this spot?
How can he send a message?
Advertise his lot.

A whisper of a marching song
Carried in the air.
A memory from the future,
Faint and hardly there

The feet of other soldiers,
March to a different war,
The tune composed in years to come.
Not written yet, she's sure.

Shivers running through her bones.
Sounds her ears can't find.
Haunting notes that drift away,
Play tricks inside her mind,

Pointless death and wasted lives.
History agrees,
And Colonel Bogey marches on
Whistled on the breeze!

Unrest

Unrest settled on the air,
It hung upon the mist,
Pervasive as the fever
Persuasive as a fist

Change was starting to appear,
Collecting heavy dues
Driving good folk from their homes,
Punished for their views,

The smell of tar was cloying,
The mob was out for blood,
Fuelled by tavern gossip,
They gathered in the mud,

The printer was in hiding,
The shop they sought to burn,
Jamie stood there, broom in hand,
And fought each one in turn.

He swung it in a fiery arc,
Warrior's eyes were gleaming,
Tar was sticking in his hair,
Sweat down his face was streaming,

Joking with the hecklers,
Grandstanding the mob,
Daubing everyone with tar
He saw it as his job.

The crowd was growing restless,
They'd take him with a rush,
Then my Scottish hero
would get tarred with the same brush.

Tar brush and Bucket

The bucket and the sweeping brush,
The pistol and the sword,
The latter are more fitting.
For an English Lord.

He swung the broom most artfully.
Painted men with tar,
More used to portraits done in oils.
They would leave no scar.

Defender of the common man,
Upholder of the law
Honour bound to action,
His fighting arm is sure.

When all around is chaos,
When lawlessness abounds,
The seed to pillage others wealth,
Takes root in fertile ground.

A stronger force than honour
Holds these two together,
The traitor and the English Man
Bound as friends forever.

Back-to-back and side by side,
They will defend what's right,
A mattress full of feathers
Will help to end the fight.

A willow broom on outstretched arm,
Hot tar at its point,
Reenforced with Highland wit,
The raiders they'll anoint.

And when the fight is over,
The skirmish is all done.
The victory is toasted,
Tis just lads having fun.

Aye Lord John I've missed ye too,
Ye've been busy I can tell,
If I just insert yon brush,
Ye may sweep the floor as well!

Tar and feathers

Before the revolution,
Things started to go wrong,
Neighbour against neighbour
Feelings, pent up strong,

Pull up your stools and sit ye down.
Watch the floor for splinters,
I'll tell you how yer Grand Da
Fought to save the printers.

Cross Creek was in turmoil,
The loyalists were done,
Packing up and leaving,
With the setting of the sun.

Driven from their livelihoods,
Businesses were burned,
Whole families turned in the streets,
Their lives were overturned.

Men were tarred and feathered,
For political belief,
The mob was out for vengeance,
It would end only in grief.

Outside Simms the printer's shop,
Defending things hard won,
A kilted red-haired Scotsman, Me!
With a broomstick Having fun!

I swept an arc with bristles,
A broom in either hand,
As I once held a broadsword,
To defend a far-off land.

Hot tar dripping from the broom,
I daubed a few in jest.
The great and good of Cross Creek
Weren't mightily impressed.

I taunted them with humour,
My mind I spoke aloud,
Tar broom flashing playfully,
I flirted with the crowd.

Distraction was what's needed,
To aid the printers flight,
Enter Ian and Fergus,
To defend the right.

The contents of a mattress,
Feathers swirling through the air,
Landing on the tar-stained crowd,
Sticking everywhere.

A shotguns blast, rings overhead,
A man runs for his life,
Twas just Isiah Morton
Being hunted by his wife!!

So, when ye have a pillow fight,
Spill feathers round yer room,
Beware of Grand Da, hunting
With the tar pot and the broom.

Twenty Rifles

Loaded on the wagon.
Gifted from the Crown
Paid for with my hard-earned coin,
I could na let him down.

Bird will have his rifles,
Tested, cleaned and bright.
Twenty will nae win this war.
Nor even win one fight.

My part of the bargain kept.
The Crown would add a twist,
The King requires loyalty,
An oath is on the list.

I can no longer hold my line.
Walk between the fires,
I fear I must tell him now,
That most white men are liars.

Bird, my women have the gift.
They see what time will bring,
A time of death and sorrow
But not brought by the King.

In sixty years, it comes to pass,
The trail on which they cried,
Sent to land so far away,
In thousands they will die.

Tell it in your stories,
Keep all this in mind,
When the time approaches,
Please be hard to find,

Wise old Bird will sing this song.
Its words will keep them free.
Sons and then his grandsons
Will hide the Cherokee,

This wife of yours, you value her.
Bird asked the question bold.
She cost me nearly everything,
Her price was more than gold.

Now the time to make the move.
To step across the wire,
March with freedom, March with hope.
Step into the fire!

Boys will be Boys.

Boys will be boys; they like a prank.
When better than on Sunday,
Cause chaos for the preacher,
Make a much more fun day.

All the Ridge turned out to hear,
Roger Macs first preaching,
Even some of Catholic faith,
Turned out to hear his teaching.

They thought it went unnoticed,
When they let the serpent out,
A brightly coloured king snake,
With a red and yellow snout.

Himself was sweating, nervous,
Standing with his wife,
Him and snakes have history,
Since one nearly took his life.

It's slithering towards him,
Underneath the people's feet,
Twill causes some consternation,
If it climbs up on a seat,

The sweating warrior draws a breath,
Hopes his nerve won't fail,
He stuffs it swiftly down his plaid,
A good grip on its tail.

The snake is wriggling wildly,
Trying to escape,
Its head pops out above his shirt,
It tries to make a break,

Our hero is now ashen,
But trying to keep calm.
Composure sure is difficult.
With a snake wrapped round your arm,

Cool, calm and collected,
Claire will take control,
She stuffs it in her pocket,
Before it can reach its goal,

A crisis is averted,
And the sinners will repent,
Roger Mac will see to that.
He saw the whole event.

The Blazing Shits

They never miss a Sunday,
Not seen for a week
Five wee bairns and counting,
They lie there cheek to cheek.

Crows circle the cabin,
Flies buzz round the door,
The heavy cloying scent of death
Creeps across the floor

Dysentery, the blazing shits
For this there is no cure,
Save wash and boil the water.
The rest you must endure.

Sickness in the water,
Find the cause, we must.
The graveyard fuller every day,
The reaper is not just.

Whole families lie dying,
Wracked with griping pain.
The body tries to purge itself.
Wants to be whole again.

Thirst and dehydration
They drink what made them ill.
Death's circle is a vicious one.
Bad water, it will kill.

I am fed up with funerals,
Of grieving for the lost,
We keep on boiling water,
And count the human cost.

Fever

A child as young a Jemmy,
A father wracked with grief.
I fell amongst the mourners,
Like an autumn leaf,

Exhausted, weak, failing,
Fever boiled across my brain,
With sparks of white-hot lightening,
Harbingers of pain.

My skin was tight and brittle,
flesh had burned away,
Pounding blood rang in my ears,
My body baked like clay,

Throat is tight, I cannot breathe,
I cannot take in air,
Faces, voices come and go,
But do not stop and stare,

I reached up and I touched it,
The beam above my head,
My fevered mind reminds me,
It's eight feet above the bed.

I hear voices calling.
I must obey them all.
Golden eyes the same as mine,
Implore me heed the call.

Braced against the window,
His face lit by the dawn,
Tears of grief run down his face,
A man prepared to mourn,

I only know I love him,
But I don't recall his name,
The amber voice still draws me in,
Will she win the game.

A figure stands beside him,
Her actions draw my eye,
That touch spurs my decision,
I'm not prepared to die.

Scales of pain

Delirium and fever,
A snake inside my brain,
Scales of red not healing blue
And never-ending pain.

I saw all things in shadow,
Yet crystal clear as day,
Dry the heat that seared me.
Foreboding here to stay

A serpent lives inside my home.
Reptilian, sly and sleek,
It spreads a poison through our lives.
Not time to turn a cheek.

I saw you at the window.
Bottle in your hand,
Helplessly I saw her there,
I saw her make her stand.

Do I know you, Jamie Fraser?
Must I spell it out,
Remind you I'm not from this time,
I cannot cope with doubt,

Cards upon the table now,
For I must be quite sure,
If she comes near my family,
I shall kill the stinking whore.

We will ride a wave of hate,
Vicious rumours spread,
Truth will out, it always will
But someone will be dead.

Sorcha

Sorcha, Claire, you are my light.
Illuminate my days,
Without you there is nothing
All in darkness stays.

You are my dawn; you are my dusk.
My winter and my spring,
You give my world a purpose,
You are it's everything.

When bleak stones held me captive
The sun would rise each day,
Each morning I was thankful.
I did'na let ye stay.

I'd watch the world about her work,
Feel what love had cost,
Hidden from me by a veil,
Gone but never lost.

She goes about her business,
Revolving through the years,
If we lose hope, all we have left,
Is bitterness and tears?

For you are all around me,
I thank the Lord for that.
I hear ye cursing to yerself,
And talking tae the cat,

And here ye are all skin and bone,
And I a worn-out wretch,
Still Ye'd take me to yer bed,
Oh, flesh of ma flesh.

Din'nae leave me Sassenach
I'd be angry should ye die,
For then all hope has left my world,
Without good reason aye.

A Cool Haircut

Don't look in the mirror Claire,
You'll surely have a shock,
They've scalped you like an Indian would.
They have nae left a lock!

Would ye like a hat now Sassenach,
Tae cover up the mess,
That would stop me laughing,
Ye look funny I confess!

Shorn just like a highland sheep,
At least yer heid is cool,
Now put that knife down Sassenach
Din'nae play the fool!

A kerch makes ye respectable,
A hat would hide the crop.
I'd love tae see ye wearing.
Some lace perched on the top.

I would na care if you were bald,
Your beauty is inside,
Your still the Claire I laid with
When ye were a bride.

Pardon me for laughing,
But ye really are a sight,
Shall I get yer scissors?
And try tae put it right.

Would ye like a whisky
Before ye have a look,
Short hair could be a fashion,
No – do not throw that book.

Kindly stop yer laughing,
You are irritating Scot,
Hair will grow when it's cut off.
I bet your balls will not.

Jamie – go and do some work,
Tormentor of my soul,
And take your hats and ketches.
And cram them up yer hole.

He floats.

He is the devil's spawn.
Pipes a child's voice.
A babe set in a basket,
He had little choice.

He floats.
The current takes him,
Drifting in the race,
Spinning in the eddies
Gathering in pace

Rising
From the water
A monster from the deep
Strong arms hold him safe and sound.
His life will not be cheap,

Child
I baptise thee,
The father and the son,
His name is Henri-Christian,
And he is mine for one,

Protection
Would you harm a child?
Baptised for the Lord,
Harm him and I'll damn you all.
Roger gives his word.

Touch him.
He is flesh and blood,
Human just like you,
And remember that God watches,
All you little heathens do.

Wisdom of Solomon

Himself
He laid his parlour out.
Tables set with care,
The choices and the consequence
Not one would he spare.

Sinners
Lined before him.
Faces white with fear,
The poker turning in the ash.
Glowed white, their skin to sear.

The Choice
The voice was calm, words dripped in ice,
Would turn their bowels loose,
Touch the bairn or touch the fire,
Tis up to you to choose,

Step Up
Watch, he is a boy like you.
He gurgles and he grins,
Make him smile, look after him,
He is innocent of sins.

The Message
One by one they touched him.
Saw him smile, and laugh,
A baby in a blanket
His size different by half.

Remember
He is a child of God.
Do this all will be fine,
And remember Henri Christian
Are also kin of mine!

Consequences
They stood in line, hearts quaking.
The consequences dire,
Lesson learned; they filed out.
Not one had touched the fire.

And….
Germaine he is your brother,
He will need your protection,
Look after him, always.
Shield him from rejection.

The Word
He said we would be damned to hell.
Baptised him for the Lord ….
Mr McKenzie – is a man of God.
Do not doubt his word.

Reward
Wisdom is a fine thing,
There's risk and there's reward,
And there is bread and honey.
With the Bible and the sword.

Faecal matter

With jar in hand, I braved the walk.
Tom Christie had the same,
Headaches and dry fever
Our guts did not inflame.

A prudish over pious man
Of women he was shy,
He thinks I do not know my place,
Thinks I come to pry.

Shorn of crowning glory
Hat upon my head
He looked at me as one he thought.
Had risen from the dead.

Enquiring of his welfare,
I went into his lair,
And ask him for a sample,
I baited gods own bear.

How dare I be so personal?
It's as if he doesn't shit,
Would he put some in my jar,
He'd have none of it!

Madam I will take you home,
I will not have this talk,
You are weakened from the fever,
You can hardly walk.

I know you mean no harm in it,
This very strange request,
You will examine nought from me.
I think ye need more rest.

Woman you are unseemly,
Your hair shorn like a monk,
What you ask is much too much.
I fear you might be drunk.

I crammed my hat upon my head,
It's angle I arranged,
Tom Christie proudly walked me home.
Some men will never change.

Mortality

Will we share some years of peace,
To watch the family grow,
The ridge to thrive and prosper,
The answer – I don't know.

Will we pass our dotage,
Rocking on our stoep,
Watching life through rheumy eyes
Our diet based on soup.

Long nights by the great room hearth,
Listening to the weather,
Long days watching seasons pass,
Growing old together.

I can'nae see that Sassenach,
Yer days are always packed,
With birthing's and wi surgery
And yer garden - that's a fact.

And I'm not much fer sittin'
Despite my creaking bones,
As long as ye keep mending me,
I shall not leave ye alone.

I promised when we married,
That I would keep ye fed,
And always with a place tae sleep,
If not always a bed.

As long as I have strength in me,
Tae get up from my seat,
As long as I can fire a gun,
The family shall have meat.

Sassenach we will get old,
We cannot stop the time,
Let's face it now, the two of us,
Are surely past our prime.

Our lives have seen much conflict,
More than our share of war,
Each night I hold you close to me,
I know we will endure.

A life force strong still drives us,
And given better weather,
We'll still ride up the mountain side,
Tae make love in the heather!

To watch ye work keeps me alive,
Yer constant quest for life,
The healing force within ye,
The witch who is ma wife!

What was it Adewayhe said,
When yer hair is white,
Your power then for healing
Will set the world alight.

Hold me Jamie Fraser,
Before we face this day,
I need your arms around me,
As dawn comes out to play.

I think I could do more than that,
I may just make ye smile.
With some luck I'll make ye squeak,
And moan in quite some style,

Now quit yer thinking of our age,
For that is but a number,
As long as we have life and breath,
We shall not choose endless slumber.

Always and forever,
In some shape and form,
Bodies joined in Union,
As we see another dawn.

Seeing Double

When it comes to finding husbands,
Lizzie causes much ado.
A quiet and hard-working lass,
You'd think there'd be a queue.

Mc Gillivray the gunsmith,
Fiancé number one,
Slept with a whore and caught the pox,
He left town at a run!

Then Young Bobby Higgins,
Would have tried his case,
But Mr Wemyss won't entertain.
That brand upon his face,

The Beardsleys her protectors
Won't see her come to harm,
There's two of them identical,
Is that cause for alarm.

For Lizzie is alas with child,
The dirty deed is done.
Is it Kezzie or Josiah,
She must marry one!

All called to the 'speak a word.'
Himself is in a rip,
Make an honest woman,
Or He'll sort it with a whip.

Three young minds together,
Are too much for the Laird.
Married one and hand fast two.
The three of them are paired.

Time is a great healer.
Folk gets used to much,
And Lizzie Wemyss lovelife
To all is double Dutch.

Unconventional

Freezing cold, we made the trip,
Barrels to the stash
Came the sound of sobbing,
In the bushes near the cache.

A wilted, drunken figure,
There sat Joseph Wemyss,
Drunk on young raw spirit,
In the ruin of his dreams,

Slung on Jamie's shoulder,
Like the carcass of a deer,
To be warmed up by the fire,
The truth we got to hear.

His daughter Lizzie is with child,
The father isn't known,
Well, she knows it's one of two,
The Beardsley twins! We groan.

Jamie's spitting feathers,
Both of them Ifrinn!!
Gaelic muttered furious,
He calls both brothers in.

Himself intends to 'speak a word.'
The matter will be sorted,
Lizzie will be married,
Before she has been courted,

She cannot name the father,
Says she loves them both,
Refuses to take one of them,
Himself lets out an oath!

So, they drew straws for her honour,
Kezzie has a wife,
Jo must make himself a ghost,
Until there is new life.

Handfast before witnesses,
And before long a priest,
The wean will have parents,
He's seen to that at least.

What goes on between them,
Of that he'll was his hands,
Two lads in just one body,
Is what Lizzie understands!

Gallberry Ointment

Mistress ye were all away,
The Malaria came on,
My teeth were clacking fit tae break,
I needed something done.

The twins they know my ointment,
And they know what to do,
Rub it in all over,
Mistress I tell ye true.

Gallberry is such smelly stuff,
They could'na stain their sarks,
So, they took their clothing off.
Preventing stains and marks.

I was cold, they kept me warm,
"Twas comfort in their touch
Mistress I was fevered.
Did I enjoy myself too much.

I woke and saw his chest, all hair.
Soft and curled like down,
Mistress it was lovely.
Please mistress do not frown.

His paps like tight wee raisins,
Right before my eye,
I never felt so safe before,
Oh, mistress please don't sigh.

I can'nae tell the difference.
Two bodies and one soul
And yes, it was the both of them.
They are what makes me whole.

Oh, Lizzie you must make a choice,
Or you may face a scandal,
Mister Fraser will take action.
If tis more than he can handle.

Keeping a lid on things

I have na felt like this in years
My heid boils fit tae burst,
Christie's first, now Beardsleys
Which ones are the worst.

Keep yer temper Fraser,
Will not do to lash out,
You may wish to throw yer fists,
And feel the need tae shout,

Ye set yerself as man in charge,
Here your word is law,
Take a breath, and count tae ten,
Then search your inner store.

Anger calm and surgical
Like Claire would use her knife,
Find a cure with cutting words,
It may preserve a life.

All may yet be straightened,
With Lizzie and the lads
Ye, see she loves both Beardsleys.
Can both of them be dads.

Ye said yer peace, ye made yer point.
And then they found their priest,
The best they could short notice
"Twas Roger Mac at least.

I can'nae kill the both of them.
And lay them at her feet,
They've pulled a fast one on the Laird,
Their solution is quite neat.

I think I can'nae worry,
it is nae worth the time.
Far worse things will happen,
Is theirs such a crime.

If we stay whole throughout this mess,
For I can hear deaths drum
I need my anger all intact
To fight what is to come!

What's a bit bigamy,
In the realm of all these sins,
And ye can'nae tell the difference.
Between the Beardsley Twins

Unholy Trinity

A furtive knock in darkness,
Three figures in the night,
Seeking out a minister,
To save them from their plight

They have a plan; it just might work.
Though himself has spoken,
Catch the preacher unawares.
Only just awoken!

Please marry us, pleads Lizzie
I find myself with child,
I do not want a scandal,
The mistress will go wild.

Kezzie is our witness.
Please marry me and Jo.
I'm sure of what I'm doing.
I really love him so!

It will nae be a marriage,
But I'll handfast ye tonight,
It's a binding union.
Tis valid in Gods sight.

But let me put my breeks on,
I've no time tae prepare,
I can't conduct a wedding.
While my arse is bare.

A trinity unholy,
Most masterful of schemes
Both twins are in the eyes of God
Hand fast to Lizzie Wemyss!

Lessons in the snow

The traits of male anatomy
Are designed for having fun,
Ye can do things that a lass can't do,
I'll show ye – this is one.

Jemmy and his Grand da
Outside in the snow,
The privy – na we'll not get there,
It is too far ye know,

They came in stamping off the cold,
Warming by the flames
Conspiring in that way of theirs,
Grand da teaching him new games.

Come and look outside he nagged,
I've learned to write my name,
So that's what Grand Da's teaching him.
He's getting all the blame.

Well now! No one listens anyway,
To what I ask them to,
And I've only taught him something,
That a lassie can'nae do!

Chaos in the Kitchen

Cookie batter in the bowl,
Jemmy waved the spoon,
Grandma can I lick the bowl?
Can I do it soon?

Batter all around his face,
Cookies in to bake,
Jem announces he has lice,
That was the first mistake,

Brianna's search for crawlers,
Lice, in Jemmy's hair,
The smell of burning treacle,
Drifting through the air,

Pulled swiftly from the oven,
Cookies fly across the room,
Adso on the hunt for them,
Stalking in the gloom!

Jamie's burnt his finger,
His pain announced in Gallic,
Holding up a finger,
In a gesture which is phallic.

Chaos in my kitchen,
Go Adso catch some mice,
We are about to shave some heads,
The men and boys have lice!

Head lice

Wee crawlers, hiding in his hair.
Young Jemmy he has lice,
Picked up from the fisher folk,
I didn't check them twice,

Sit ye down my little man,
Time tae cut yer hair,
Yes, I fear it will be short,
Just like granny Claire.

His lovely locks fell to the floor,
With lice they were alive,
Crawlers running for the door.
Clean up on aisle five!

What is this mark upon his scalp,
A nevus small and red,
Just above his wee left ear,
A mole, here on his head.

It's nothing tae concern ye,
I'm sure I have one too,
Growing here under my hair,
I was five before it grew.

They say they are inherited,
A coin begins to fall.
This shows that Jemmy is my son.
Now no doubt at all.

Sit down Roger brave the shave,
You two can look as one,
Shorn like sheep, and granny Claire.
A father and his son.

Dear Jamie/Dear John

Dear Jamie, Since I've known you,
You've had scant care for rule.
In God's name do not do this
Tis the action of a fool.

Stubborn and intemperate
Tell me that you're not,
Honourable, intelligent,
Foolhardy, reckless, Scot!

Named again a traitor,
A known seditionist.
Denounce these rumours Jamie please.
They have you on their list.

Your family endangered,
Don't play fast and loose,
The only end that I can see.
Is your neck in a noose.

The Crown will send its army,
Your cause will be suppressed,
The King will have his justice,
You surely face arrest,

For sake of ties between us
And history long gone.
Reaffirm your loyalty,
Yours in friendship - John

Dear John, your letter comes too late,
my course is set tis plain,
I'd not put you in danger,
I shall not write again!

I sever ties between us,
With the greatest of regret,
Your humblest Jamie Fraser,
P.S they have nae caught me yet!

The Plan

Brother you were always there.
Yet I sense you do me wrong.
It is not right the things you do,
Yet I play along.

Father will not suffer this.
It was not in the plan,
I fear I am got with child,
And yes – you are the man.

Fraser, he has money.
Lure him to your side,
He is a man, he won't resist,
Soon you could be his bride.

Betray his wife, she is a witch,
We can see her dead,
Once she's gone, he'll claim his child.
That's more jam for our bread.

So, I watched and waited,
Collected what I'd need,
The way he took his woman.
His passion in the deed.

When you've lived a life of lies
The truth is hard to see,
No way in god's universe
Would he lie with me.

I knew the script, I learned it well,
I backed it up with fact,
A mire so deep in evil
I never can retract.

Allan plays the outrage,
I play the wounded soul.
Comfort in his darkest hours
My heart as black as coal.

Stiff with white hot anger,
Quiet pent-up rage,
This man who offered kindness.
Stepped onto the stage.

He called my lies; he called me whore.
I nearly lost my nerve,
He promised I would tell the truth,
Or get what I'd deserve.

A Warped Mind

Who knows the depths a mind can plumb?
When it comes to schemes,
This child I'd taken to my trust,
Had schemed beyond my dreams.

A web of lies so complex.
It sounded like the truth,
Complete in minor detail,
Which in her mind was proof,

A bid to take my husband?
To ruin people's lives,
I could feel the gossips,
Sharpening their knives.

Her father – rightly angry,
Her brother – fit to kill,
Jamie – livid to his core,
Malva – lying – still.

I found her in my garden,
Throat slashed with a knife.
Her babies heart still beating,
I tried hard to save its life.

Only time will find the truth,
Our lives are put on hold,
To serve a warped and twisted mind,
And someone's thirst for gold.

Shamed

Congregation hear her!
She does not tell you lies,
False tears running down her cheeks,
Her innocence defies.

Seduced by one she trusted,
One who should have cared.
One who promised kindness.
Looked for how she fared.

She does not name her lover,
Not before this crowd
The lie is told to him alone,
His name she speaks aloud.

Her words are truth, as spoken.
If you know the man
But will mislead and will cause pain.
It's all part of the plan.

Her baby is a bastard,
It will not bear a name,
The man who is the father,
Cannot announce his claim.

A brother who looked after her,
He who should be kind.
Who nursed her as a baby,
A sinner we shall find.

In anger he protests too much,
He makes too much demand.
His jealousy of Frasers life
Will overplay his hand.

She would not maintain the lie,
Her life pays for the truth,
Mind tormented, filled with guilt,
She'll sacrifice her youth.

Her father has suspicions.
The lies he cannot stop,
But deep inside he knows the truth,
We hear the penny drop.

Superstition

Gripped in superstition.
Fear of the unknown,
The seed of hate is planted.
And soon enough it's grown.

Deep in soil of ignorance,
Watered then with doubt,
It pokes its shoots up to the sky,
A weed you should pull out.

Choking truth, like bindweed
Propagating fear
It sees just what it wants to see.
Here's what it wants to hear.

Healing becomes witchcraft.
Good deeds become a crime,
Stubborn and reliant
On tales from olden time.

Every slight is magnified,
Every fault is grown,
Fingers point and tongues will wag,
The gossip weed is sown.

Where is knowledge when you need her,
To know the hearts of men,
And the wicked tongues of women,
Whose talk is cheap – ye ken.

They will sit around their kettles.
Throw snippets in with pride,
What they knew of Malva
The facts will be denied.

They covet all that has been built.
Envy fuels the flame
Religion the accelerant,
To destroy the Fraser name

For every truth there is a lie,
For every lie a reason.
No evidence to prove a crime,
The Fraser hunting season.

Toil and Trouble

I came upon him in the woods,
The man they call Himself,
I wandered, picking mushrooms,
Stealthy as an elf.

He does not know I watch him,
I see his every move,
My mind's eye maps his body.
Covets every groove,

He is a man of honour,
He would do what's right,
He could be led into our trap,
Would he even fight.

My wiles could draw him from her,
Send her to the grave,
Be his comfort in his grief,
Then he'd be my slave.

Sister this is not the plan,
Tis I you take to bed,
The child is mine, you are mine,
no more to be said.

I loved you since you were a bairn,
We saw our mother die,
Who cared for you in those dark times,
Who heard your every cry.

Father tried to change you,
He tried to cleanse your soul,
Listen well and serve the Lord.
Always hide our goal.

I would get us free of him,
Live our lives alone,
Without the pious ranting
His loud religious drone.

Sister you must not be swayed,
Commit the lies to mind,
Smallest detail proves your case,
See what you can find.

Father then and mistress,
Fevered like to die,
I'd comfort Mr Fraser,
Pursue the darkest lie.

My sinfulness is then revealed,
In words so meek and mild,
I'll only tell this to 'himself.'
I'm carrying his child!

I'd watched him in the river,
Bathing with the men,
That tiny scar upon his arse
That was the one ye ken.

That fine lean muscled body,
Bears scars he wears with pride,
But that wee one, cannot be seen.
Tis hidden from the eye.

A bite scar soon forgotten,
A small knot in his skin,
Will prove to some I tell the truth,
But have I lain with him?

Ringing in the Ears

Do my ears deceive me,
Lies are all I hear,
Corroborated clever lies,
Trouble brews, I fear.

How dare she speak of him like this,
My right fist starts to cramp,
She's spread her legs for someone else.
Morals of a tramp,

Lying scheming alley cat,
Her brother eggs her on,
Her father must believe her,
And he must believe his son.

'Sir how could ye treat me so.'
'He could not get enough.'
So, help me shall I slap her now,
Or wait for his rebuff.

The arm that wields the pestle
Unleashed from my control,
All my strength behind it,
Landed on its goal.

A little out of practice,
Long since I threw a dish,
I haven't slapped a living soul.
Since Jamie with that fish!

I set her ears ringing,
My throwing arm unfurled.
Released a sound that Outlanders.
Would hear around the world.

Trouble in Spades

We would see her buried,
Would see her soul with God.
They would lay her body.
In unconsecrated sod.

I would wash her sins away.
I would sew the wound.
I would wrap her in her shroud.
To lay her in the ground.

They would spread the rumour.
They would twist the truth,
Say I wash my guilt away.
Along with Malvas youth.

We will hold a service,
Roger will say prayers.
They will say I am to blame.
Corrupting one of theirs.

Circumstance against me,
The evidence is scant,
But all believe us guilty.
I've nothing to recant.

Hiram Crombie spread his seeds,
Word poison sewn with care,
He will not speak them to your face,
He would never dare.

Action and reaction,
If Allan is so shocked
Why take the coffin to your breast,
Your arms around it locked,

Malva was your sister,
Reaction says she's more,
Why are you weeping for her child?
Yet call its mother whore!

The truth will shame the devil.
Time will bring the proof.
Meanwhile trouble comes in spades,
And heaps it on our roof.

A Moments Rest

Voices hide in cupboards.
Ghosts invade the air,
I hear them, and I look for them.
I see they are not there.

My helper calls,
my faithful mask
A moments peace
Is all I ask?

I cannot face this music,
Too much in my mind,
Sweet sleep and oblivion
My refuge I must find.

A few sweet drops
Upon the mask
I will find my peace.
At last

Am I old and withered,
That she would have my life,
This house, my home, my everything
She wants to be his wife.

Devoid of life
Her body lies.
Her throat laid open wide.
Face to the skies.

There is no happy ending.
Someone wanted blood.
And Malva Christie's body
Lies lifeless in the mud,

Murdered
Life taken.
All will be.
Mistaken

The child lives, I see it move
I can save its life.
Surgery in the garden
With a pruning knife

Elbow deep
Blood and shock
Malva on
The butchers block.

Not a pretty picture
They will not understand.
Demented woman murders child
The blood is on my hand.

Bolt the Door – again.

He heard it first, the rumble.
The hooves across the ground,
The clink of harness and of guns
A distant chilling sounds.

I saw his eyes flash steely blue,
Unreadable his mask,
Intruders come into our life,
My defence his task

Pulled up outside rifle range,
That voice rang in my ears,
This committee is not safety,
It brings my greatest fears.

The gloating words, the challenge
Enjoyment in our strife,
Richard Brown announces,
That he's come for Frasers Wife.

My wife is not a murderer,
Ye will nae take her in,
It's not her crime tae answer for,
This is not her sin.

No evidence but gossip,
No proof but idle chat,
Ye are nothing but a lynch mob,
A vengeful one at that.

Load the guns now Sassenach,
Tis time tae go to war,
And for a different reason,
It's best we bolt the door!

Rough Justice

Malva was already dead,
I tried to save the child,
Denigrated as a witch,
The Browns would hold a trial.

This is revenge, not justice,
Tis all about his brother,
That and petty jealousy,
Mob justice has no honour.

Under guise of safety,
No reason and no law,
No evidence presented,
They'd lynch us that's for sure.

And so, begins a journey,
Helpless at their hands,
Victims of the Christie's
But not one understands,

Easy to condemn a man,
His honour to impugn,
Easy to shout, 'burn the witch.'
My work forgotten soon.

At least we go together,
Two of us, are strong.
What is this Tom Christie,
Is it for justice you're along.

A deep one is Tom Christie,
He knows I'm not a witch,
There is method in his madness,
On a rope we shall not twitch!

Scales of Justice

I cannot see this woman hanged,
Her skill before it's time,
Is healing wounds and curing ills.
Really such a crime?

I do believe in witches,
She is not one of those,
She has a rare intelligence.
A calling I suppose.

And he inspires loyalty.
Men follow him to die,
A man of honour bound by truth.
I've never known him lie.

And then I fear I know my son
A weak and snivelling liar,
A sneak thief and a coward
won't set the world afire.

Jealousy lives in his soul,
He has no sense of pride,
Envy curdles all his deeds.
And gnaws at his inside.

And then I know the devils get
Her blood is of a witch,
Her mother was a sorceress.
My wife the whoring bitch.

The Lord will see that truth is out,
The devil put to shame,
Papist, Presbyterian
Our God is one – the same.

And should the Lord be tardy,
In putting things to right,
I will see that justice.
Fights the Frasers fight.

A man who takes a flogging
To spare one mad and old,
Whose wife returned in all those years,
Would never break his code.

An educated woman,
Duped by the witch's mind,
Has walked into the fire of hell.
Her kind heart made her blind.

The Ridge is made of simple folk.
They fear the unknown
Superstition justifies.
The evil seeds they've sown.

Brown would have a hanging.
He has vengeance in his soul,
A personal vendetta
The gallows are his goal.

Tom Christie looked into his heart.
With love where all else fails,
He added truth to justice.
And balanced up the scales.

Only I can heal this wound.
Be the bigger man,
I must step in Frasers shoes,
And fill them if I can.

Surety

Innocence protested,
Death the Browns had planned.
Tom Christie entered in the fray,
And offered out a hand,

Justice his if anyone's,
Malva was his child,
He would see us safely,
There would be a trial.

His hair unkempt, his beard long
He walked an old man's walk,
But took command and saved our lives,
Made sense and justice talk.

One last night in our own bed
Under our own roof
He'd escort us then to Hillsboro.
And a trial to find the truth.

Jamie still would fight the world,
And all that that entails.
This man of words who spoke with sense,
Took wind from all Browns sails.

Tom Christie was our surety.
To him it would ensure
There would be no lynching.
Before our guilt was sure

The start of a long journey,
To try and prove our case,
Now living in a lawless land,
Where justice hides her face.

Taken

Shutters closed! Bolted tight,
Bar behind the door,
Rifles primed and loaded.
Kept beneath the floor.

We could hold out for hours,
Maybe not for days,
Food and water rationed.
We shall see how this one plays.

Richard Brown seeks justice.
No, he seeks revenge.
He blames me for his brother's death,
And that, he would avenge.

He stands there waving flags of truce.
His tricorn in his hand.
I'd shoot that hat from off his head,
Before we leave this land.

I mark the line with rifle fire,
A line he will not breach,
Come no closer, lest ye die.
Step into rifles reach.

Hiram Crombie offers words,
The Fisher folk are come.
But burn the witch is all they want,
By the pricking of my thumb.

Burn the witch, avenge the lass,
Bring out yer murdering wife.
Verdict reached without a trial,
Claire would lose her life.

And Allan Christie eggs them on
Seeks vengeance for his kin,
I think that he protests too much,
Not devoid of sin.

Loaded in a wagon,
Taken from our home,
Where are the folk we needed,
Now for Justice we must roam.

Gone

Jamie!
Overpowered,
He fought, there were too many,
Then a gun butt to his head,
The world went black around him.
Then I thought him dead.

Jamie!
Do not take him.
You said we'd go together,
Liars all, you bastards,
You won't defeat us – ever.

Tom
Where is my husband,
Is he still alive,
If he is dead, there is no hope,
I cannot survive.

Trust Me
Mistress Fraser,
He looked into my eyes,
Trust the Lord, trust what is right,
I will not let you die.

Find Him!
No! I stay with you,
To you I gave my hand,
He is alive, I know him well.
Survivor to the end,

Tom
What are you not telling me,
Tell me what they've done,
Tell me where they've taken him.
Or I really can't go on.

Days on days the wagon drove.
Looking for the law,
Broken towns and broken lives,
We saw the start of war.

Now bars and locks and darkness.
Will they break me, I can't tell?
My mind goes back to Wentworth,
A prison, yes, and hell

I fight with you.

There was but a second.
Before the world went black
When silent death, swift as the wind
Started our fight back.

Planning to deport me,
To Scotland – on that ship,
Losing Claire and losing life
Losing every grip.

Light on the air and silent
They rained their arrows down,
Christ Ian lad ye took ye time,
My breeks are turning brown.

Bearkiller, now we fight with you.
Browns henchmen on the sand,
Cherokee with rifles,
Chief Bird makes a stand.

So, there is another day,
The fight will still go on,
Can ye tell me someone, please.
Where my wife has gone.

Bodies on the Beach

I followed unseen as a ghost,
A leaf caught on the breeze,
Hidden in the shadows.
Of the forests and the trees,

Always at a distance,
But always there in case,
When their last card has been laid
Then I show my face.

A ship lay out at anchor,
Not far from the beach,
My uncle tied and hooded.
Browns men in easy reach.

Watch and wait and bide our time,
Til they drop their guard,
Then the silent arrows fly,
Then we go in hard.

I've Chief Birds rifle on my right,
I ride between two fires.
On my left, come to our aid.
Is big John Quincy Myers.

Ye shall nae steal my uncle,
He will not cross the sea,
I've others watching Aunty Claire
She's where she's s'posed tae be.

Richard Browns committee
Is riding for a fall,
This time I give the order,
And we will kill them all.

Staying Alive

Midwife, servant, forger,
The Governor needed all,
His wife with child, his clerk left town.
I'm at his beckon call.

Our faces on the broadsheets
Cause more than some ado.
We'd be the entertainment.
On gallows made for two

Convicted forgers always hang.
Imagine my elation!
And murderers can claim the church.
If they have an education.

I wrote the note with stolen ink.
Stolen parchment, stolen quill,
I hoped he'd find out where I was,
If I was here still,

Then the move to Brunswick
Dressed as the governor's wife,
My prison now the Cruizer
But At least I have my life.

I sleep, I eat, I work, I write.
I hear the watches change,
Sailors' footsteps on the deck,
The voices of the strange.

I feel him near, he hunts for me.
Will he find my trail?
If not, I am all at sea,
And my ship has lost his sail.

He will come Today.

A forger or a murderess
What will become of me?
I lean upon the deck rail.
I stare out to the sea.

I copy letters faithfully,
I watch and wait and pray.
My mind sees every boat leave shore.
He will come today!

Today is gone, there is no sign.
Meanwhile I survive.
I have no word, but in my soul.
I know he is alive.

Long sure strokes, Bent to the oars.
I know that form so well.
My lifting spirits call to him.
He comes to end my hell.

Brooking no resistance,
He bargains for my life,
Making legal argument
He comes to claim his wife.

Poker faced, he hides his cards,
He knows his hand is weak.
Little here to bargain with,
No aces, so to speak.

He fights public opinion,
The rope must feel our jerk.
The broadsheets spread in every town.
Have really done their work!

He argues that in martial law,
I could be set free,
The Governor won't take a bribe,
Parole is not to be.

A canny man the Governor,
His bargain is for men.
Two hundred, back woods highlanders,
To swell his army then.

Discretion is the getter part,
The player takes command.
Asks time to think upon the deal,
Before he shows his hand.

In Gaelic tongue he says farewell
Says he will return,
I know his promises he keeps,
So, in my hell I burn.

Morning comes, there is a boat,
Rowed by a different hand.
My sinking heart in turmoil,
Tom Christie takes the stand.

A hurried conversation,
Confession sworn and signed,
Admitting what he did not do.
His honour is that kind.

He has thought this over,
The broadsheets soon will tell,
How Malva Christie's father,
Damned her soul to hell.

She was his brother's daughter,
His voice ne'er missed a stitch.
The brother who took Christie's wife
Who bedded Christie's witch?

A broken child, who learned her trade.
Who planned it from the start,
To kill her father and myself
Then capture Jamie's heart.

I left him there upon that ship,
A prisoner of his mind,
Sworn to put the matter right,
His love for me that blind.

The Jamie Fraser guide to Prisons

Fort William is local,
Escape is not too hard,
The whipping post is well used.
And convenient in the yard,

The food dry bread and water,
The company is poor,
Chickens are much better,
And I'm used to them for sure.

Wentworth is a doozy,
Tis fifty to a cell,
If ye get a dungeon
Then they torture ye as well,

There are hangings every morning,
Ye'll not escape the noose,
Ye don't get out of here alive,
Ye will not be turned loose.

But find the postern entrance,
Unlocked if time allows,
Ye may escape under the guise.
Of fifteen highland cows.

The Bastille is a fortress,
It is nae very clean.
And whilst it's French they din'nae serve
The very best cuisine

Ardsmuir was the bleakest,
The rats were at their best,
They kept me there in fetters.
In case I caused unrest

The Governor could do nothing.
Without I had my say,
A Masonic lodge in Prison,
Would keep disputes at bay.

Helwater was nae prison,
Twas service on parole,
Fresh air, horses, greenery
It helped tae keep me whole.

And now I'm far from Scotland.
In a land they say is free,
But my wife has found a prison,
Will she stay there? Wait and see!

Listening from the kitchen.

I'm out in the kitchen,
He thinks I've no idea.
When he is telling stories
What those kids may hear,

He loves to tell his stories.
Sit back and reminisce,
But some are not exactly,
A gentle bed time kiss.

He tells them so completely.
In the language of the day,
He forgets that in this time of ours,
Our grandkids will not stay.

They will all go home you see,
And no one else can know.
That they visit their Grand da,
Two hundred years ago.

His language is emotive,
He has a way with words,
If a bit old fashioned,
We no longer talk of turds.

But they are learning of their family.
And how it once was riven.
And if they learn to swear in Gaelic.
Grand da, will not be forgiven.

And when it comes to cooking
I admit - I'd rather not.
If he chooses not to eat it,
I could hit him with the pot.

Get out of my kitchen.

Can ye no prevent it sir,
This invasion of ma oven,
They've filled it with the strangest thing.
And surround it like a coven.

Is ma bread nae good enough?
I'm feeding half the ridge,
And what's this cupboard full of ice.
Yer daughter calls a fridge!

She caught me in ma 'speak a word.'
And then she spoke a few,
Merdina wants her kitchen clear.
Of witches and their hue

I don't ken what they're up to
But I'd better go and see.
Whatever this creation is.
They'll try it out on me!

Smells like fresh bread baking.
I'm liking this one well.
Toasted cheese, and pickles
And is that herbs I smell,

Ah Sassenach, how goes it,
Are ye cooking up my tea,
I smelled it from ma study,
Is it all for me?

They pulled it from the oven.
This culinary beast
Twas crispy, yes, and golden brown
An aromatic feast

Like corbies aye they fell on it,
As if they'd not been fed,
The smell made ma mouth water,
This is not only bread!

Mind yer whisht now Mrs Bugg,
They are not brewing spells.
Just experimenting
With stimulating smells

Cut up into slices,
eaten from yer hand.
The modern lack of cutlery
I'll never understand.

Yon thing it comes from Italy.
Like the Bonnie Prince ye say?
Mark me! This looks more useful.
I think I'll let it stay.

I've never seen two women.
Eat with so much glee.
Ladies, please, I'm starvin'
Will ye leave a bit fer me!

Burgers for Tea

Made in Brianna's cabin,
With Roger we both schemed
Tastebuds craving modern food,
Of which we only dreamed.

I think we could make burgers,
The kids should have a treat,
And after all their Grand Da
Just shot half a ton of meat!

I'm sure that there are off cuts,
Bits that we can grind,
The patties are the easy bit,
The cheese is hard to find!

And Mrs Bug will question.
If I start making bread,
Interrupt her baking.
I may well end up dead.

Then there is the ketchup,
Tomatoes for a sauce,
There's plenty round the privy,
Not poisonous of course!

A tasty feast of bison
Served up in a bun,
Himself would find it challenging,
To watch him would be fun.

So, we all sat round the table.
For Fraser Burger night
Red hair in abundance
But not a clown in sight

I like this better Sassenach.
It does nae cloy ma teeth,
And with a bit more practice
It might just taste of beef!

Spaghetti Tree

What is it that she's making,
Wi flour, eggs, and oil,
Must be some new remedy,
But why rolled out in a coil.

Och no, now she's boiling it.
Are we having it for tea,
Is anybody nervous?
Or is it only me.

Once she showed me tape worms,
Pulled from someone's arse.
There is some similarity,
On supper I may pass!

Spaghetti is it Sassenach,
And tomatoes in a sauce,
I'd rather bread and honey,
If convenient, of course.

And how will ye explain it?
To bairns who are not Brees,
Shall I take a dish outside?
And hang it on the trees.

Ye could send them out tae pick It,
Make the process fun,
I see the little heathens.
Gather pasta by the ton.

At least I'd have some warning.
And there is one last question,
Is yer culinary effort.
Going tae give me indigestion.

A side of chips too far

How can you eat a burger?
If you have no fries,
This may be a challenge.
Best avert your eyes,

Potatoes dug fresh from the ground,
Peeled and cut in strips,
It's hard to cut them thin enough,
I guess we'll stick with chips.

Sunflower oil, will take the heat,
We need a source of flame.
Don't set fire to the house.
I hear you all exclaim.

Take great care now Sassenach,
With trouble will ye toil,
Why are ye cutting tatties up.
And boiling them in oil,

Mrs Bugg is on ma case,
And it does'nae smell too fine,
Tis bubbling like the devil.
She fears ye've crossed the line.

There's cooked and then there's crispy.
Claire, I din'nae think ye've learned.
Cooking things with witchcraft
Will get my supper burned,

It does nae pay to play with fire.
The devil ye may poke,
Fer goodness's sake forget the chips.
Fore we all go up in smoke,

This time I put my foot down,
Please listen my wee mouse,
In the lifetime I have left take me
I'll not rebuild this house!

PB & J

I will not let the kids grow up,
Without tasting peanut butter
Claire declared some weeks ago,
What's that? She heard me mutter.

The table laid for supper,
The family gathered round,
What is this dish she's serving?
No one makes a sound!

She's cut the bread in slices,
And then stuck them back together,
Eating this new-fangled thing
May be heavy weather.

I look around the table,
Folk are eating with their hands,
That's not what I was taught to do,
I'm not sure I understand!

Well in I go, I'd better taste,
This thing that's made of bread,
Ken, I'll stab it with my fork.
Best make sure it's dead.

It tastes like nothing natural,
It wraps around yer teeth,
I could fix my shoes with this,
And what's this underneath?

It's sickly sweet, and sticky,
But I'd much rather honey,
Ye can keep yer peanut butter,
I'll nae be wasting money.

Ye could use it tae seal letters,
Or glue back things that's damaged,
But I will no' be eating,
Another peanut, jelly sandwich!

Dreamscape

I dreamed I saw ye Sassenach,
Ye sat there framed in light,
I did'nae ken how old ye were,
Yer hair, it was'nae white.

I felt that Ye'd been writing.
Ye had that studious look,
The one ye get when things ye've done.
ye write them in yer book.

I can nae say twas in yer past,
My dreams go where they will,
I could dream tartan flutterbys,
But they will no' keep still.

Do I dream our future then?
See things that will be,
Should I die, then you must go.
You, the bairns, and Bree.

Ye ken I can nae keep ye safe,
If all around is war,
Promise me that you, at least.
Will step back through times door.

One last stone, tis all we have
One stone can take ye back,
Tis the colour of the future aye,
One stone, a diamond, black.

Why would I go, when all is here,
My life is built with you,
This family, this time, this life
I'd stay and see things through.

There's nothing now beyond those stones,
I've sacrificed my time,
Don't think you can be shot of me.
Because I'm past my prime.

He placed that diamond in my hand,
He begged me not to stay,
I'd rather die than leave him.
I threw the stone away.

Together we will ride the storm,
And if we can survive,
Home is here and in this time
And for now, we are alive

And if you have that dream again
You aggravating Scot.
Please tell me if the butterflies,
Have tartan wings or not.

Forbes Ear

Brianna had been taken.
Held on Bonnets craft.
Kidnapped by the lawyer,
Is Neil Forbes quite daft.

He sat there in the parlour.
Enjoying a strong cider,
Self-satisfied, and gloating
She's where no one will find her,

A hand upon his shoulder,
Brings him back to life,
Roger Mac, a grip of iron.
Where sir is my wife.

Forbes denies all knowledge,
Rogers eyes a laser,
Ian Murray with a knife.
But where is Jamie Fraser.

Jamie is off picnicking,
He's calling on Forbes mother,
A kidnap is a grand day out,
He charms her like no other.

A messenger, a note is sent.
A brooch as proof of deed,
Forbes spills all to Roger Mac,
To get his mother freed.

Bonnets ship Anemone
Set sail for English shores.
Brianna as a cargo,
Along with slaves and whores.

Her father would have searched for her.
Far across the seas
Forbes problem with James Fraser
Instantly would cease.

Roger springs plans a rescue.
Forbes has cause to fear,
Ian's knife is swift and sure.
In cutting off Forbes ear,

A talisman to find her.
The Mohawk way, he grins,
And a reminder to a lawyer
Don't mess with Fraser kin!

Talisman

Tradition of the Mohawk,
When searching for a foe,
Always have a talisman
To guide you as you go.

A talisman should find you,
Tis an object which reflects.
The aura of the subject,
It's target it selects.

It could be the strangest thing,
But will focus all your mind,
Clear your thoughts to see the task.
Take away the blinds.

The spirits they were calling.
When I took Forbes's ear,
This was my cousins Talisman.
It heard her calls, her fear.

Roger raised an eyebrow.
Uncle Jamie, well he joked.
Asked if it was salted well,
No, I said - it's smoked.

He looked at it with horror.
Before he could enquire
In the kitchen at the in
I held it o'er the fire.

We will find Brianna.
The spirits make it clear.
Tucked inside my sporran.
A wood smoked lawyer's ear.

Mistress Forbes Picnic

Mistress will ye dine wi me?
I giggled like a child.
A courtly bow, a cheeky grin
I looked at him and smiled.

My wife has left me wanting,
She's gone off tae a birth,
I saw the sun glint off his hair,
Laughed for all I'm worth.

My! he is a handsome man,
Well mannered, so polite.
Why should I not go with him,
Would Neil not think it right.

Mistress I'd steal ye away,
To picnic 'neath a tree,
The weathers fine, as is the food,
You'll surely come wi me!

One hand on the basket,
He swept me up like dust,
Drove me in his carriage,
And over me he fussed.

I saw his blue eyes twinkle,
He flirted and he'd flatter.
Courtly manners to the fore,
His words a silken patter

Why would Mr Fraser want,
A lady such as me,
I am older than the hills.
Have more wrinkles than his tree.

I had such fun that afternoon,
Nothing did, I fear.
But what on earth had Neil done?
That he should lose an ear.

Chowder and Marching

Send two Scotsmen shopping,
I've given them a list,
And very strict instructions
Not to come back pissed!

They've goods to trade, they've goods to sell.
And on the list a fish,
Something edible and large
Is that too big a wish.

Cinnamon and needles,
Pepper, salt, and pins,
Don't get into mischief,
There's no prize for more sins,

Blackened eyes and laughter,
Ripped clothes flap on the breeze.
Battered men and battered fish,
An explanation please!

A minor disagreement,
A scuffle on the dock,
The fish was swung at someone,
Gave him quite a knock.

Ian has his finger,
wedged tight up his snout.
Stifled groans of laughter,
His brain may well fall out.

Don't send two Scotsmen shopping,
Twill start off with a brawl,
And end up with a stolen gem,
Stuck where it can't fall.

I'm going in with tweezers,
I've really had enough.
Before I can, these fighting men,
Have shifted it with Snuff.

Aaaaaaaachooooooo!

A verra English Uncle

Sit still ye braw wee heathens,
Before ye trash the house,
Creep ye softly down the hall,
Quiet as a mouse.

Did ye see the panel,
Ripped from side to side,
The Redcoats did that one fine day,
When I'd come tae hide.

We left it thus, so all can see.
The damage caused by conflict,
The mindless acts of damage caused,
When looking for a convict.

Not all English men are bad,
A few have saved my life,
And yer Granny Claire's a Sassenach,
Yes, I have an English wife.

And you have an uncle,
You may find him in a book,
He is 9th Earl of Ellesmere,
You may want to take a look.

He may never come tae Scotland,
He does na feel his roots,
He is my son, and just like his da,
Gets too big for his boots.

If ye should ever meet him,
Just look in the mirror,
His likeness to yer ma – and me,
Just might make ye shiver.

Raised to be a gentleman,
A wealthy English Earl,
It's better that he stays away,
From the Pipers Skirl,

But I'd give my mortal soul,
Yer Gran Da's not a liar,
To see my Willies English boots,
Stood by my Scottish fire.

Come Sassenach, join us here,
Come out of yer lair,
Pour a dram and raise a glass,
To a verra English heir.

Meeting on the Dock

Disembarking soldiers
Chaos on the dock,
Another day in Wilmington,
An unexpected shock.

Brianna on a mission,
Is mercy in her head?
Or is her purpose really.
To make sure Bonnets dead.

Who is that with Lord John Grey,
He surely looks like Da,
But Da dressed as a redcoat,
Too farfetched by far.

He has his height; He has his grace.
Lord John what a surprise,
Who is this copy of my father,
Damn, he even has his eyes.

His Lordship consternated.
Flapping like the birds
Seeing my mental penny drop,
Explains his loss of words.

Helwater, seventeen fifty-eight!
And yes, your mother knows,
He must not see your father,
My suspicion grows.

Yes, you have a brother,
Please don't let him see.
He can't know he's a bastard,
Do this thing for me Bree.

And so, I met my brother,
Greeted him as friend,
Knowing sure as eggs are eggs.
He'll find out in the end.

Blood will out

William Lord Ellesmere,
Handsome and a flirt
Chatting up the ladies,
And all things in a skirt,

Commissioned in the army,
A lieutenant oh so dashing,
All red coat and epaulettes,
And then the sabre flashing,

Brought up the old-fashioned way.
A very English charmer
Birds fall from trees before him.
Girls cannot hide their ardour.

Behind the polished manners,
A twinkle in his eye
A remnant of his childhood,
His parentage of lies,

A natural way of being,
A humour in his words,
This did not come from charm school,
Or talking to the birds,

An innate human kindness
To care for those he loves,
To see the best in women,
And treat them with kid gloves.

Rachel – sees right through him,
He is not quite her thing,
She's fallen for his cousin,
That rebuff will sting,

Jane – he loved her dearly,
Her soul he tried to save,
Too late to stop a mortal sin,
Now she is in her grave.

And Amaranthus Cowden.
Another cousin's wife,
Asking you to marry,
Just to save a child his life.

Some things you will learn from life.
Some things you are taught.
Take a lesson from yer father.
These dalliances are naught.

Try and find the right one,
Before your seeds are sown,
Wait until you feel that love,
That many have not known.

You are loved by many.
On both sides of your life,
Do not be in too much haste.
To find yourself a wife.

Bastard though you may be.
Your true blood is as blue,
It oozes out through all your pores,
The natural Scot in you.

Unrepentant

I cannot see this as the end,
I've always found an out,
Irish luck runs in my veins,
Of that I have no doubt.

A morbid fear of drowning,
Strange for one like me,
Captain of a smugglers ship
Who lived a life at sea.

I was not brought up honest,
I've lived my life in sin,
Now I'm paying for it,
My tide is coming in.

Every man I ever robbed,
Every man I maimed,
Every woman that I raped,
Every life I claimed,

Measured now in water,
Life's cloth is wearing thin,
I cannot fight against the tide,
And now it's coming in.

Every penny stolen,
Every cruel deed,
Every soul thrown to the sea,
When there was not a need.

Measured now in inches,
As it rises, should I grin,
Or fight against these shackles,
The tide is coming in.

Every last deception,
Every lie I told,
Every man I led to think.
I was not out for gold.

I feel the water rising,
It's now up to my chin,
God will know my prayers as lies.
And the tide will still come in.

The red haired one forgave me,
Offered me a way,
I tried to use her kindness,
I regret it to this day,

Well, I regret that I was caught,
Regret I met her father,
You will not twice deceive a Scot,
Sure, it gets them in a lather.

I've no more time for thinking,
I cannot breathe – ifrinn.
Blarney will not help me now,
The tide is nearly in.

I've pissed myself, My bowels void,
I'd rather I'd been hanged,
My tide of life is surely in,
And now it's over .... BANG.

Conspiracy Theory

The letter began 'father.'
Ominous from the start,
Then Willie started to outline
The feelings of his heart!

In love with Dorothea!
Lord Greys feelings lurched,
Encounter in a garden,
Honour now besmirched!

Marriage to his cousin
Hal will not stand for that!
These two are conspiring,
But what is it they're at?

He says he loves her dearly,
That is not William's way,
He's not a great romantic,
There is something else in play.

I question Dorothea,
Her honour is intact,
As is her virginity,
She tells me this as fact!

She pleads her love for William,
His gentle loving soul,
His fine good looks, enquiring mind.
This story is not whole!

Have I not been a diplomat,
Employed to save a nation,
Can I not tell when youngsters?
Use prevarication.

With Willie in America
There is time to sort this out,
But Dottie's schemes get her, her way.
And that's without a doubt.

I will get to the bottom,
Before the plot gets silly,
Dorothea has plans to get wed,
But I'll bet it's not to Willie.

She'd travel to the colonies,
Where William fights a war,
I sense she has a goal in mind!
Who does she travel for?

I must talk to her father,
She lays the flirting thick,
Women's wiles hard at work
She doesn't miss a trick.

And Hal will reap the whirlwind,
A fathers will she'll flout,
Best I tell him gently,
It's no good for his gout!

Michael Mouse

Who is this, Walter Disney?
Where is this strange place,
Where children learn of fairy tales,
He does'nae show his face!

Don't they have their chores tae do?
Or learn to use a knife!
How have they time to waste on things,
On leisure in this life!

I've been told this land is happy,
That children love to go,
And play there with the characters,
A giant puppet show.

They should play in the mountains,
Run upon the hills,
Climbing trees and hunting things,
Learn practical skills,

What are moving pictures?
What is a theme park?
Why this fascination,
For sitting in the dark?

I've been told of technology,
Man will fly to the moon,
I'm not sure that I understand,
The need to go so soon!

My grandson is a canny lad,
He lives across the years,
But when he travels through the stones,
It vexes him tae tears.

He must be brave, like Grand Da,
When he leaves our house,
And if he gets to see him,
Give my best tae Michael Mouse!

Telephone for Grand Da

Basic Anaesthetics,
Basic equipment too,
Operate on Mandy
Something I cannot do!

She needs the care of experts,
She needs a special op,
Complex surgery on her heart,
To make the murmur stop.

As soon as they are able.
I know that they must go,
Back through the screaming dark abyss
And we will miss them so.

And so they went, we said goodbye.
Prayed they made it safe,
Back to modern medicine,
To save Young Mandy's life.

I woke alone from restless sleep,
He was outside in the air.
he said had been dreaming.
And they all were safely there.

He'd seen a town like Inverness,
Described to me the Manse,
A study with long windows,
A kind wee brown-haired lass,

An object on a table,
With a club shaped like a bone,
And a tail just like a curly pig.
Is that a Telephone.

Jemmy lifting up the club,
Calling from afar,
Long distance and two hundred years,
Phone call for Grand Da!

Lost Soul Remembered

You learned, I taught,
You schemed and thought,
You planned and you betrayed,
I trusted you,
I cared for you,
All that was false you played.
I still can't see you evil,
Though all around me do,
Even at your violent end,
I tried to rescue you.

You learned my ways,
You learned his too,
You looked into our life,
Was it really in your plan,
Evict me – as his wife.

Oh, child of rare intelligence,
For no one is born bad,
I found out from your father.
The start in life you had.

Endless curiosity,
Was all of it a sham,
You think he would have kept you,
My honourable man,
Another child that is not his,

Was it all part of your scam.

You truly thought of everything,
Except that grain of good,
The one seed that was in your soul,
To treat me as you should,

You tried to put it all to right.
Refused to follow through,
You died for that,
I know that now,
Your brother murdered you.

Your soul lies in my garden,
Buried in the weeds,
Your body in the graveyard,
Where it cannot plant more seeds.

I still come here and think of you,
Your child I could not save,
My lessons about saving lives,
Near sent us to our graves.

You never saw the hatred,
When they came to take us down,
Lives destroyed one fiery night,
At the hands of Richard Brown,

You sent us on a journey,
Which should end in a noose,
Released a tide of anger,
Which never should break loose.

But we are back,
We are as one.
And stronger than before,
Battered at the edges,
Forged harder by a war.

Our bond is one you could not break,
It is not of this life.
Time itself has not the power
To split him from his wife

Home Raiders
31st December 1776

They came in search of jewels,
They searched and then they wrecked,
No thought, just mindless damage,
And no point to object!

All the jewels we had are used,
Our family is gone,
Donner wants his passage home,
Cannot believe we've none.

Smash of glass, and China.
In shards on the upon the floor,
Windows broken needlessly,
Our home wrecked and what for?

Knife to my throat, demanding,
They can't see it as truth,
They'd murder for the hell of it,
They're unwashed and uncouth!

Jamie spins a ripping yarn.
I'm the only one who knows,
Where the jewels are really hidden,
There is ether in his nose.

The Bugs come home to chaos,
The Big House torn awry,
These raiders have not realised,
They are about to die.

The ether flask is broken,
Sleep creeps across the floor,
Creeping fog, explosive death,
Will end this raid and more!

What's this in Merdinas bag,
Hidden in her knitting,
A Fleur de Lys stamped bar of gold,
They have the rest I'm betting.

Stupor over takes them,
Anaesthetic gas,
Sends the raiders off to sleep,
It's not the end, alas.

Ian and his Indians,
Have come to save the day.
But do not light that candle,
Please turn and run away.

Ian NO! I scream at him,
He's reaching for the matches,
Brianna's bright invention,
Will sign off our dispatches.

A ball of fire across the room,
Remaining windows blow,
We run before the fireball,
Our legs are far too slow,

Farewell house, goodbye nice things,
Poverty returns,
The clothes that we stand up in,
And superficial burns!

All is not lost, forever,
Before he gets too old,
Jamie will extract the truth,
Of where Arch hid the gold.

But that's another chapter,
And life goes on for sure,
Back to the cabin in the woods,
And sleep upon the floor.

We are alive! He writes it,
Our house is charcoal sticks,
Sending news, from New Year's Eve
Seventeen Seventy-Six

Sworn Vengeance

Greed runs deep in some men.
And some can bear a grudge,
Stubborn as the meanest mule,
Their minds you will not budge.

Rather take what they believe.
Should have been their due.
Than ask, they'd think it 'cap in hand.'
And that would never do.

We had kept watch in snow and rain,
Winter on the ridge,
Could not have been much colder.
If we'd had a fridge.

(What is a Fridge Sassenach?)

Arch had sent his good wife back,
To steal the stash of gold,
Buried underneath the house,
Where the Sow lives with her brood.

Merdina fired the pistol,
Ian saved my life,
An arrow deadly accurate,
Killed Arch Bugs good wife.

You should' na send your woman.
To carry out yer plan.
It's your fault that you lost her,
Don't blame another man.

You'll take away what Ian loves,
And ye'll follow him for years.
Ye'll wait until he finds her,
And then you'll cause him tears,

A bitter man, with half a hand
And only half a life.
Old, and nothing left to lose,
Will he avenge his wife?

The Coming Storm

It's nice to have a normal day,
One without a drama,
Boring domestic humdrum
Seems to make me calmer.

There's heavy weather coming.
I hear the distant thunder,
Lightening forking from the sky,
A divine signal, I wonder.

I know unrest is coming.
There will be a war,
I know that he will fight it,
Of that I know, I'm sure.

I will pack up and go with him,
Be an army wife.
I could not bear to lose him now,
This man who is my life.

Jamie and Claire's Theme
Alternative words to the Skye Boat Song

Time will flow on,
When we are all gone
Our love will never die,
Two hundred years
It will always be strong.
Two souls as one my dear

Blood of my blood
Bone of my bone,
Travelling down the years,
Holding you close
Feeling you strong
Smoothing away your fears.

Time will not dim.
Years will not age
Your beauty will never die.
Sassenach Lass here in my arms,
Forever and e'er to lie.

Ghostly I came,
Calling your name
Hoping you'd be my soul,
Spirit in chains,
Purgatory claims
True love will keep us whole.

Blood of my blood
Bone of my bone,
Travelling down the years,
Holding you close
Feeling you strong
Smoothing away your fears.

We will go on.
Til all life has gone
A love that does not enslave
Powerful love as lasting as ours
Truly transcends the grave.

Acknowledgements

As always, my first acknowledgement is to the written word of Diana Gabaldon wo has been the inspiration for all these poems and rhymes. Acknowledgment also to the makers and cas6t of the Outlander Series.
Also, to Diane Riddell who has allowed me to use one of her photo edits as the cover for this work.

Copyright

The right of Maggie Jenkins to be identified as the author of this work has been asserted by her in accordance with the Copyright, Designs and Patents Act 1988. All characters and events in this publication are fictitious and any resemblance to real persons, living or dead, is purely coincidental.
"All rights reserved. No part of this publication may be reproduced, stored in a retrieval system, or transmitted in any form or by any means without the prior permission in writing of the publisher, nor be otherwise circulated in any form of binding or cover other than that in which it is published without a similar condition, including this condition, being imposed on the subsequent purchaser. A CIP catalogue record for this book is available from the British Library

Other work by the author
The Author has also written a series of books of poetry based on the Outlander Television Series:

Unofficial Droughtlander Relief.

The Droughtlander Progress.

Totally Obsessed.

Fireside Stories.

Je Suis Prest.

Après Le Deluge

Dragonflies of Summer

Semper in Aeternum

Sia air Ochd

Intervallaqua

Facing the Storm

The Blue Vase

Mille Basia Volume 1

These are also sold to raise money for RDA – If you are a fan of the series try them, they have received some excellent reviews from purchasers.

I hope the Princess will Approve – a book of COVID and Horse related poems.

Ginger like Biscuits - the adventures of a Welsh Mountain Pony. – a short book written for young teenaged horse enthusiasts.

A recipe for disaster - poems about the authors life.

All are published through Amazon.

Or sold through the authors Etsy Shop poemsandthings.

Email: chestyathome@aol.com

Printed in Great Britain
by Amazon